Marzollo, Jean

Getting your period

$13.95

DATE			

GETTING YOUR PERIOD

A Book About Menstruation

GETTING YOUR PERIOD

A Book About Menstruation

Jean Marzollo

illustrated by
Kent Williams

introduction by Marcia Storch, M. D.

Dial Books for Young Readers
New York

A NOTE TO THE READER

The ideas, procedures, and suggestions contained in this book are not intended as a substitute for consulting with your physician. All matters regarding your health require medical supervision.

Published by Dial Books for Young Readers
A Division of Penguin Books USA Inc.
375 Hudson Street
New York, New York 10014

Printed in the U.S.A.
Design by Nancy R. Leo
First Edition
E
10 9 8 7 6 5 4 3

Library of Congress Cataloging in Publication Data

Marzollo, Jean.
Getting your period: a book about menstruation
by Jean Marzollo; illustrations by Kent Williams.
p. cm.
Includes index.
Summary: Discusses the facts and feelings about menstruation citing the experiences of individual girls of different ages.
Also includes descriptive illustrations.
ISBN 0-8037-0355-4. ISBN 0-8037-0356-2 (pbk)
1. Menstruation—Juvenile literature.
2. Adolescent girls—Growth—Juvenile literature.
3. Adolescent girls—Health and hygiene—Juvenile literature.
[1. Menstruation.]
I. Williams, Kent, ill. II. Title.
RJ145.M37 1989 612′.662—dc19 88-3986 CIP AC

The artist was assisted in the research for the illustrations by Sherilyn van Valkenburgh.

Dedicated to my friends Rita Brown and Sarah Crane, with love and appreciation for their outstanding work in the field of health.

Contents

Introduction

This book explains what happens when you start to grow up. It describes the changes on the outside and the inside of your body and the changes in your feelings. As children all of us watch older girls becoming adolescents and we know that we too will change. But when? And how?

How different will I look?
How tall will I get?
How big will my breasts grow?
When will I get body hair?
When will my period come?
How different will I feel?

Size, shape, and emotions are not easily predictable, and this may be confusing or make you anxious. An older sister may be helpful, but what if you don't have one, or what if *you* are the older sister?

Girls in this and many other countries are brought up to be much more private about their bodies than boys. Boys are expected to dress and undress together and to compare themselves with one another from an early age. The current expansion of women's team sports is making this locker-room experience available to more girls. I hope it will result in greater openness and better information about periods and puberty.

In 1972 when I began to run a gynecology clinic for adolescents, I looked for a book like *Getting Your Period.* Since then, many times a year someone asks me to recommend a book for young adolescents. It has been hard to do so because most authors write for parents or for older teenagers. Jean Marzollo has very successfully filled this important need.

This is your book. If you can read it—it's for you. The facts are correctly and directly explained. It also shows you that there is great variety in the process of growing up both physically and emotionally. You will learn that although you are an individual, you are not alone.

I wish *Getting Your Period* had been published twenty years ago, and I hope that in twenty years you will be giving a newly revised edition to someone as old as you are now.

Marcia Storch, M.D.
Obstetrician/Gynecologist
New York City

GETTING YOUR PERIOD

A Book About Menstruation

1 / Getting Your Period for the First Time

Getting your period for the first time is an important event in your life because it is a sign that you have changed. For some girls the change is wonderful and exciting. For some it is scary, and for still others it is a little of both.

This book will help you sort out your feelings and find out what's going on—not just in your body but in your mind too. What's happening to you is similar to, yet different from, what happens to others, because no two girls are exactly alike. There is no perfectly "normal" way to have your period. Instead there are lots of normal ways, and your way is one of them.

In this book different girls who menstruate (MEN-stroo-ate) will share their knowledge and experience with you. They'll tell you how they feel about it and what they do to cope. Whatever your feelings, you'll probably find that other girls are just as pleased, indifferent, or upset as you are.

The word *menstruate* and the phrase *getting your period* may embarrass you at first. Calling your period your "friend" and "the curse" doesn't help much, but at least these odd phrases, used by many, convey a little feeling. Sometimes getting your period can feel like a curse, and calling it your "friend" adds a touch of humor to a situation that often can use it.

The roots of the word *menstruation* (men-stroo-AY-shun) lie in the words *measure, moon,* and *monthly. Menstruation* means "moon change," and in Germany some people call their periods the "moon." This is because women get their periods roughly every twenty-eight days, the same length of time it takes the moon to complete a cycle from new moon to full moon and back to new moon again.

Your menstrual cycle, like the moon, is part of nature: interesting, mysterious, and occasionally a little intimidating. It helps to know as much as you can about it.

Anticipation

Before girls start their periods, most know that it's coming. Some feel excitement and joy; they can't wait to do something so "grown-up." Others feel only dread. The thought of blood, cramps, tampons, and bodily change make them want to run and hide. Many girls don't particularly care one way or another.

Some girls are shocked when they first see spots of blood on their underpants. Either no one told these girls about menstruation or, when someone did, they weren't paying attention. The information presented may have been too abstract for them to comprehend, or maybe they just didn't feel like listening. Their attitude may have been: "Someday I'll need to know about that, but I don't want to know about it now, so I won't listen." Whatever the reason, the surprise can be frightening.

> When I saw the blood, I thought I was cut and wounded. I couldn't imagine how it had happened, and I didn't know what to do.

Such fears can be alleviated by girls' knowing about menstruation ahead of time. But even if they know about the topic, girls still vary in the extent to which they want to discuss it. Some like to talk with their friends, sisters, aunts, and parents about what they think menstruating will be like. Others feel more private and prefer not to talk about it until they start.

Since no two girls are exactly alike, the actual experience of getting one's period varies from girl to girl.

I was fourteen. I was sitting at my desk and felt sort of funny, and I knew I had gotten it. I was home with my younger sister, so I didn't say anything to her. But a close friend of mine had gotten her period earlier, and she had told me about it in the greatest of confidence. She made me promise to tell her when I got mine, so I called her right up. When my mom came home, I told her. It was great; I felt really good. At first I used pads all the time, but after a year Mom bought me tampons.

When I first got my period, I was eleven. I noticed it when I went to the bathroom and there was blood on my underpants. I called my mother, who helped me with everything. I felt excited and proud, but I basically had to keep my feelings to myself because I was on a trip in another country and I couldn't talk to my friends at home.

I was nine when I got my period. I hated getting it. I didn't tell my mother or my sister. I just put toilet paper in my underpants and tried to pretend nothing was happening. A few days later my mother came to me and said she was doing the wash and noticed stains on my underpants. She called me into the bathroom and gave me a box of pads. She must have had them ready. She showed me how to use them. I was so embarrassed, I thought I would die.

I was fourteen, and it was summer. I was on a camping trip with my family. I went to the bathroom and noticed it when I wiped myself. I felt shaky and scared. I told my mother what had happened. She got slightly emotional and hugged me. Then she helped me use something for it. I was really disgusted, and I still think that menstruating is an incredible pain.

I was thirteen when I got my period. I had an awful stomachache the whole day and had to miss my music lesson. I didn't know what it was until I went to the bathroom. I was kind of happy I had finally gotten it, but I also knew it would be a drag. My older sisters helped me with it mainly, and no one ever teased me.

I was eleven, getting ready for a Little League game. When I sat down on the toilet, I noticed a brown spot on my underpants. I thought I hadn't wiped myself well enough before. Then, when I used toilet paper, I realized something was definitely there. I was only in the fifth grade. I had a game to play. What if that stuff got on my uniform? I was sitting there wondering what to do when my little brother started banging on the bathroom door. "Go get Mom!" I yelled. I must have scared him because for once he did what I told him to do. Mom seemed happy. She showed me what to do and said not to worry about the game. "What if I get that stuff on my uniform?" I asked. But she said not to worry. She said there wouldn't be very much blood since it was my first period.

I was twelve. I went to the mall with my older sister and her friend. They went off and left me, so I bought myself an ice-cream cone and walked around, looking for kids my age. My underpants felt kind of weird and damp, but I didn't really think about it. Then I realized what was happening, so I finished my ice cream and went to the girls' room. I was so happy! I bought a pad in the girls' room and found my sister as fast as I could. She and her friend were really nice to me.

Though the stories are different there is something similar about them: Each girl was surprised when her period actually came. It makes sense when you think about it. Since there's no way you can ever know exactly when you will start menstruating, the first time will most likely be a bit of a jolt. No matter how you feel about it ahead of time, the reality of seeing your blood and knowing you will continue to menstruate every month takes getting used to.

You might have noticed that all the girls quoted here remember quite vividly what happened to them the day they started their periods. Try an experiment. Ask your mother, aunt, baby-sitter, camp counselor, or any other older female with whom you feel close to tell you about her first period. Explain simply that you want to see if she remembers and that you are curious about what it can be like for different people.

You'll probably find that the person you ask does remember because the event marked a special change in her life. In succeeding chapters you'll find out more about that change.

2 / How You Change During Puberty

Your first menstrual period is perhaps the most outstanding event in a series of events called puberty (PEW-ber-tee). To understand the relationship between getting your period and puberty, think of a stage play with several acts. Puberty is the whole play. Getting your period is one act. Other acts are the other changes that occur in your body during puberty, such as getting pubic hair and developing breasts.

During puberty your sex organs develop and mature. Your sex organs are those parts of your body that enable you to reproduce, or have babies.

Ever since you were born your body has grown

in special ways at different times. Within days after you were born, your eyes developed because you needed to see right away. In the first year of your life your first teeth developed so that you were able to chew food. Now, during puberty, your sex organs are developing. Once you start to menstruate, you will be able to have a baby.

At least you will be physically able to have a baby. But puberty doesn't make you emotionally ready or mature enough to bring one up. That takes much more time. If you want to be a good mother someday, you should give yourself many more years of growing before you take on the responsibilities of parenthood.

When Does Puberty Start?

Puberty takes place in boys and girls between the ages of nine and eighteen. It can happen before you become a teenager or after you have become one. Most girls start menstruating when they're twelve or thirteen.

No one really knows why puberty starts for different people at different times, but we do know that people develop at different rates throughout their lives. There's no precise schedule that everyone follows. If you watch two-year-olds at a playground, you'll see that children of the same age vary in their ability to walk and talk. Some develop these abilities sooner than others. But by the time they enter kindergarten, no one remembers who was first because it doesn't really matter. It is the same with puberty.

> I got my period at age nine. I was the only one in my class who had it. I tried to keep it a secret.

> I didn't get my period until I was fourteen. It was embarrassing. I tried to keep it a secret that I hadn't started.

Girls who get their periods late often wish they'd gotten them earlier, and girls who get their periods early often wish they'd gotten them later. It seems to be natural for people to envy each other and to think that other people's lives are better than theirs, even though this may not be so at all.

How Girls Change During Puberty

During puberty, hormones (chemical messengers inside both males and females) signal your body to change in a number of ways. Although the timing is different for different girls, the changes usually happen in the order described below. You may have experienced some of these changes already.

1 • Body Development: During puberty your breasts, hips, and buttocks begin to develop.

These body parts develop in different ways and at different rates in different girls. No two naked girls look alike, and there is no one perfect or "correct" female shape to have.

2 • Pubic Hair: During puberty hair grows in your pubic area. "Pubic" (PEW-bik) refers to the part of your body between your legs.

3 • Sweat Glands: During puberty your sweat glands begin to function. This means that you may now produce underarm body odor and consequently have to wash more frequently and perhaps use a deodorant. More active sweat glands may cause your face and hair to be oilier than they have been. Wash them more carefully now with soap and shampoo, and rinse well with water. If you have trouble with pimples or acne, ask an older friend, parent, doctor, or pharmacist for advice.

4 • Underarm Hair: Hair usually starts to grow under your arms about a year after it has begun to grow in your pubic area.

5 • Whitish Discharge: A whitish fluid may come out of your vaginal (VA-jin-al) opening. Your vaginal opening is the beginning of your vagina (vuh-JINE-ah). For more information about the vagina, see pages 30–32. The whitish discharge that comes out of your vagina may be a sign that you are getting ready to menstruate.

6 • Menstrual Blood: A few months after the

whitish fluid has appeared, menstruation may begin with a little blood trickling out of your vaginal opening. Beginning to menstruate is one of the most dramatic events during puberty, but as you can see, it is not the only one. And there are even more changes to experience.

Other Changes

During puberty your voice may deepen a little, not as much as boys' voices do, but there may be a change.

During puberty you may grow taller. Since girls often go through puberty a little bit ahead of boys, you may find yourself taller than boys for a while, until they catch up. Try not to worry about it. Think of fashion models, who are tall, and tell yourself to stand up straight.

> My father told me to stand up straight and be proud of my height. He said the boys would catch up with me eventually.

> I was so excited when I saw a movie in which a short boy and a tall girl fell in love. It was great because I am the tallest girl in my class.

During puberty you may also gain a little weight. Some weight gain is natural and fine for your body.

If you eat too much and exercise too little, however, you may gain too much weight and may need to diet. If you do need to diet, consult a doctor or nurse for the right diet for you. Avoid fad diets; they don't work in the long run and can be unhealthy.

> Though I was worried about getting fat when I was eleven, the weirdest thing happened: I ate more than ever! I got way too fat, so my pediatrician said I had to go on a diet. It was wicked hard; but I did it, and I feel much better now.

Beware of the opposite problem. As some girls go through puberty, they get very confused about how they think their figures should look. Many girls dislike the new growth in their breasts and hips because their fuller figures make them feel fat. Such girls may compensate for perfectly healthy growth and weight gain by eating less than they should. They put themselves on diets, mistakenly thinking that being ultrathin is more important than eating nutritiously.

Undereating is dangerous; it can be as bad for you as overeating. It may lead to self-starvation, a sickness called anorexia (an-oh-REK-see-ah), from which people can die. Another dangerous eating disorder some girls develop during puberty is bulimia (bew-LIM-ee-ah), a pattern of overeating and then vomiting on purpose in order not to gain weight.

> I think I wanted to stay the way I was. I didn't want to change, and I dreaded the thought of getting fat. So I stopped eating most foods. I ate just the barest amount of food I could, and I got really thin. I knew fruit was good for you and not fattening, so I ate grapes all the time. I got diarrhea from eating so much fruit and so little other food. Finally my mother took me to the doctor, who said I had to gain five pounds in three weeks. She told me to make milk shakes with eggs in them after school. She told me to eat bread and potatoes and rice, foods I had been avoiding. She said I was too influenced by fashion. After I went to her, I saw a TV show on anorexia, and it scared me. So I gained weight, but I never got fat. I'm just right now.

If you feel that you are eating too little or too much or in unhealthy ways, you should talk about your concerns with a parent, relative, older friend, guidance counselor, doctor, nurse, or other adviser. Find someone who can help you learn to feel proud of your body and to take care of it by eating better.

Your Sex Organs: Where They Are, What They're For, and How They Change During Puberty

During puberty your sex organs change; some of these changes you can see, and some you can't. In order to understand these changes, it helps to learn through diagrams what's going on.

You have inner and outer sex organs. Your external sex organs, also called your genitals (JEN-it-tals) or genitalia (jen-it-TALE-ee-ah), include your clitoris (KLIT-tor-iss); vaginal lips, or labia (LAY-bee-ah); and your vaginal opening. These all are in your pubic area. You can touch this area of your body and see it with the help of a mirror.

Because the pubic area is normally out of view to you, you may feel shy or silly about looking at it or even seeing a picture of it, but it is helpful to know about your own body.

My mother, who's a nurse, showed me how to look at myself down below with a hand mirror. It was weird at first but sort of interesting.

I think if we wore clothes over our elbows all the time, we wouldn't want to look at them either.

I'm not shy about my body at all. I feel proud of it.

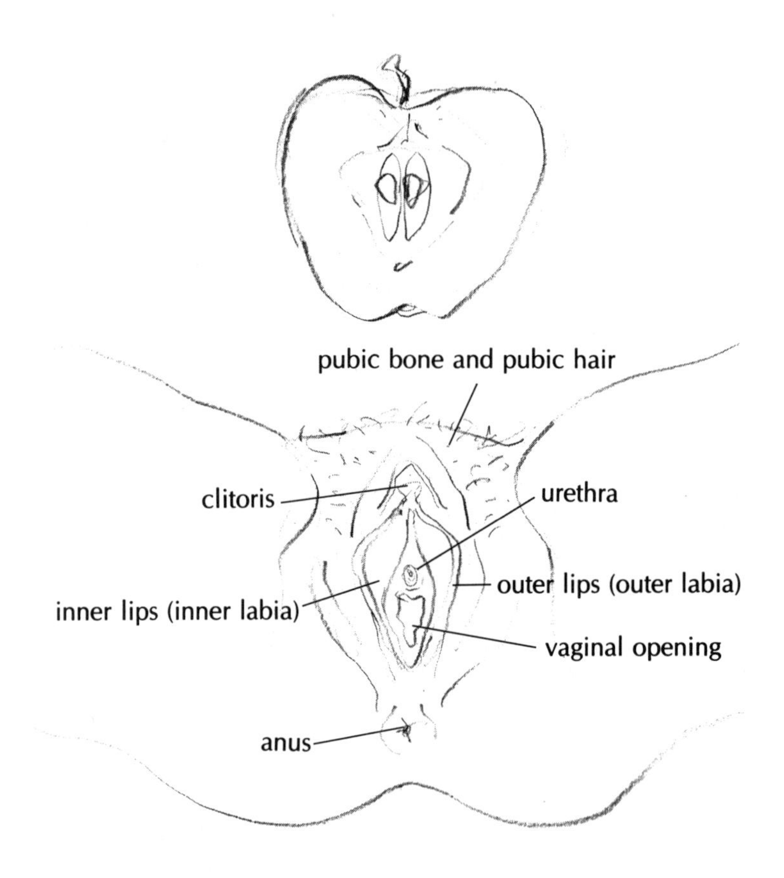

Looking at female genitalia is not so different from looking at a cross section of an apple or the inside of a flower.

Female Genitals

If you put your hand on your pubic area, the first thing you will feel is your pubic hair or the place where it will grow and, under your skin, your pubic bone. Your pubic hair and pubic bone protect your pubic area. The fat pad over your pubic bone gets thicker during puberty.

When you move your hand down, the next thing you feel is a sex organ called your clitoris, a little flap or bump of skin and nerve endings that becomes larger during puberty. The purpose of your clitoris is to give you sexual pleasure. It feels good when it is rubbed.

Next comes a very small hole, the urethra (yoo-REE-thra), through which urine passes when you urinate, or "pee." During puberty your urethra becomes larger.

Your vaginal opening, the second hole, also becomes larger during puberty. Your vaginal opening is the entryway to your vagina, an internal passageway that leads to your other internal sex organs. (Your internal sex organs are your vagina, cervix [SIR-vix], uterus [YOO-ter-us], fallopian [fah-LOW-pee-an] tubes, and ovaries [OH-vah-reez]. These will be discussed further in Chapter Three.)

Menstrual blood flows out of the vagina and vaginal opening. The vagina is also the passageway that a male's penis (PEE-niss) enters during sexual intercourse and the passageway through which a baby is born. The vagina is something like a collapsed balloon. While it is small now (you can fit your finger or a tampon into it), it is able to stretch to accommodate a baby during birth.

Around your vaginal opening are soft folds of skin called inner lips, or inner labia, and outer lips, or outer labia. The labia protect the vaginal opening; during puberty they become fleshier.

The clitoris, urethra, vaginal opening, and the labia together form an area often referred to as the vulva (VUL-vah).

Behind your vaginal opening is a third hole, your anus (AY-nuss), through which feces (FEE-seez), or bowel movements, pass.

Emotional Changes

Puberty brings about a number of changes a girl has to get used to. Some girls get used to these changes more easily than others. Some are even delighted with them. They feel that the good thing about puberty is that they are growing up, just as nature has planned. They feel proud of themselves, and rightly so. Though changing from a girl to a young woman is something every girl does, it still feels like a miracle.

> I had been waiting so long to get breasts; it seemed as if I never would. Then when I was thirteen, they began to grow and I loved it.

On the other hand, some girls feel that they are changing too fast. They may feel as if they are on a roller coaster with no brakes: It's exciting but also a little too powerful and upsetting.

My breasts grew when I was ten. I wasn't prepared for the change. They felt funny and bumpy and sore. It took me months to get used to them.

It seemed as if I had changed bodies overnight. I felt like Alice in Wonderland. It was a nightmare.

I tried to stop the growth of my breasts by wearing a cinch belt around them at night; but there was no way to stop them, so I finally gave up. But I didn't like my breasts. They were too big.

Still other girls are frustrated that their changes are not coming fast enough. They may feel that they are stuck in their undeveloped bodies and that nothing will ever change.

I tried to make my breasts grow by not sleeping on my stomach at night. I was afraid the pressure of my body would keep them from growing. But nothing I did would make them grow. I was flat as a board.

When I finally got pubic hair, I felt grown-up around younger girls, but I still felt like a baby around my older sister because I didn't have hair under my arms yet. I couldn't wait to get it.

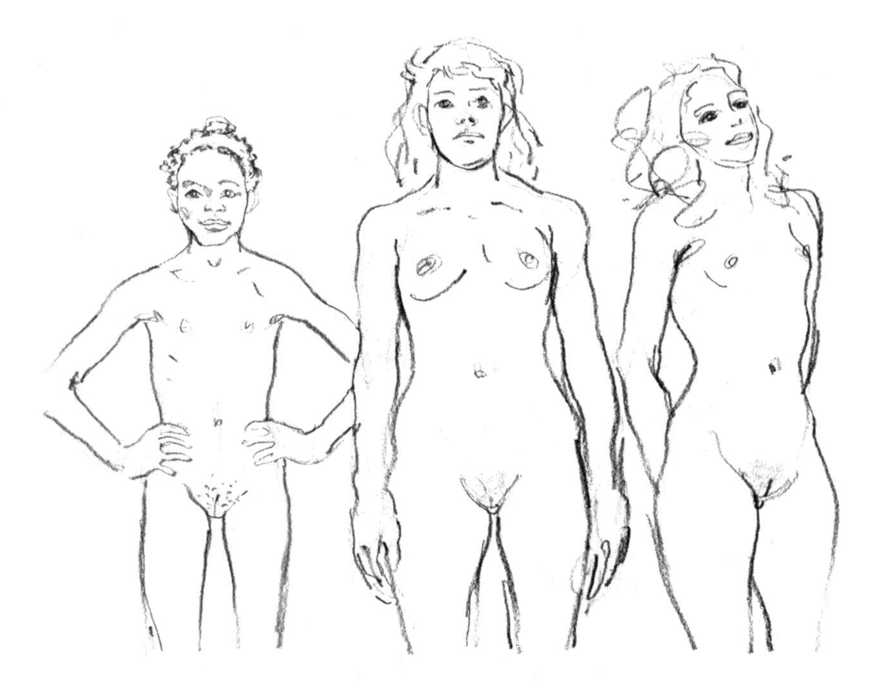

Girls' bodies are different, and they develop at different rates. All these girls are normal.

As human beings we're always growing, but at certain times in our lives we seem to grow more than at others. Puberty, for some girls, is such a time. The intense growth during puberty can lead to very strong emotions. These emotions are caused by the physical changes themselves as well as by your reactions to them.

Emotionally you may feel conflict about growing up. On one hand, you want to be a grown-up; on the other, you want to remain a child. One of the tasks of your age is to learn how to find a balance between enjoying the feeling of being more adult while enjoying the child inside you. You don't have to leave behind the child in you; on the contrary, you can take the playfulness of childhood with you into adulthood and still be serious and responsible.

You may also feel a conflict between wanting to be dependent and independent, between needing your parents a lot and not needing them at all. As a small child you needed guidance and help from your parents at every turn. As you grew, however, you became more and more able to do things for yourself. Now in many ways you are quite competent to take care of yourself, but still you can't do everything for yourself. Knowing when to be independent and when to submit, willingly or unwillingly, to authority is difficult.

Sometimes (for example, when laundry needs to be done or food prepared for supper) it's great to have a parent manage your life; other times (for example, when a movie needs to be selected or a curfew is set) it's a pain. Such conflicts over dependence and independence are normal for young people and their parents.

Getting your period means that you have to manage more things by yourself. You already manage your schoolwork and schoolbooks; now, in addition, you have to bring menstruation supplies with you to school, change them when you need to, dispose of used supplies—all on your own. It's not easy, and it's understandable that getting your period may sometimes make you wish you could go back in time and become a child again.

Another conflict you may have is the tug-of-war between wanting to be uniquely yourself and wanting to be just like others. You might like to have your own personal style of dress, for example, yet want your body to look the same as everyone else's. Here it helps to face the fact that girls' bodies are different from one another.

> I noticed at camp that everyone in my cabin looked different. Some of my friends had big breasts; some had small. My best friend had one breast that was bigger than the other! Some of the girls had a lot of pubic hair, some had a few scraggly hairs, and some had none at all. Some of the girls were plump and curvy; others were straight and skinny. We all were embarrassed at first, but then we got used to each other. What difference does it make? We're all girls!

Such differences among female bodies do not go away. Grown women have exactly the same kinds of differences. The final result of growing up is that different kinds of girls become different kinds of women, not that girls turn into women who all look the same. Wouldn't it be a boring world if that were true?

Still it's frustrating to feel you look "different." If you feel this way, it can help to realize that other girls may well feel the same way as you. It can also help to know that there are things you can do, within reason, to influence your body's shape. You can take care to eat healthfully so that you don't become overweight or underweight. Healthful meals contain foods chosen from each of the four food groups: the milk and dairy products group, the meat/poultry/fish/beans group, the bread/cereal group, and the fruit/vegetable group. Exercising regularly will give your body good muscle tone and skin tone.

Best of all you can try to stop wishing you were someone else and accept yourself for who you are. It isn't easy, and it helps to remind yourself whenever necessary that insecurities and mood swings are normal during puberty. If today you feel horribly moody and yearn to be someone else, tell yourself to be patient. Feelings that are tormenting you today may well be gone by tomorrow—perhaps only to reappear the following day, but that's a part of puberty.

3 / Menstruation

Once you've started to menstruate you can expect to get your period for a short "period" (three to seven days) approximately every month. During your period menstrual blood will trickle out of your vaginal opening.

The blood doesn't come out all at once, but rather it drips and dribbles out over several days. Some girls have heavy flows, some have medium flows, and some have light flows. Many girls experience varying rates of flow—usually heavy at first, tapering off to medium and then light.

> I have a heavier flow on the first day than on the following days.

> I have a heavy flow for several days. It's a drag, but then it tapers off.

> I bleed more on the second day than on any other.

The amount of blood that drips out varies from girl to girl, but the average is two ounces, or a quarter of a cup.

> It seems each month as if quarts are pouring out of me!

> I have hardly any blood at all. My doctor said that for some girls with very light periods, the amount may be no more than a tablespoon.

The shedding of menstrual blood is often referred to as a "loss" of blood, but it's not like the loss of blood you experience if you cut yourself. That kind of loss results from an injury. Menstrual blood is a healthy and natural kind of bleeding. As the bleeding occurs, you soak up the blood with tampons or pads, which you then discard. For more information about taking care of yourself during your period, see Chapter Four. The purpose of this chapter is to explain how your menstrual cycle works.

The Menstrual Cycle

Each month your internal sex organs work together to complete a menstrual cycle. Your cycle begins on Day One of a menstrual period and goes to Day One of the next period. The average cycle takes twenty-eight days, but most girls and women get their periods every twenty-six to thirty days. Your cycle may be shorter or longer (anywhere from seventeen to thirty-five days long).

It's a good idea to know when to expect your next period so that you can be prepared. To find out your average cycle, mark the day you start your period on a calendar with a circle or a *P*. The next time you start, mark that day on the same calendar. Keep a record of your starting days for a few months and then count how long your cycles were. Add the length of your cycles and then divide by the number of cycles. For example, if three of your cycles were twenty-eight, twenty-nine, and twenty-seven days long, add these numbers to get a total of eighty-four days, then divide by three—the number of cycles—to get an average of twenty-eight days from Day One of your period to Day One of the next.

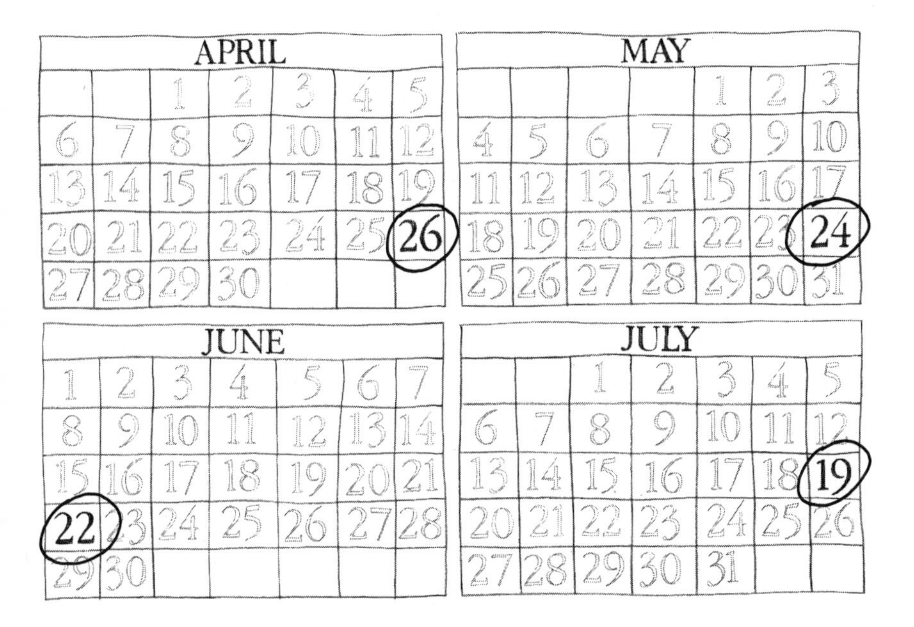

Keep a record of your menstrual cycles. Even if your periods are regular, they won't always come precisely on schedule. Let's say you have a twenty-eight day cycle. That means that on the average *your periods will come every twenty-eight days.*

Hormones, Your Menstrual Cycle, and Your Internal Sex Organs

Your menstrual cycle is managed by your brain, which sends chemical substances called hormones to different parts of your body. Hormones are like messengers that tell your reproductive system what to do. During puberty hormones tell your reproductive system to develop; they tell your breasts and pubic hair to grow, and they cause your internal sex organs to change too. Each month hormones tell your body to menstruate. To understand menstruation better, it helps to know what your internal sex organs look like and how they function.

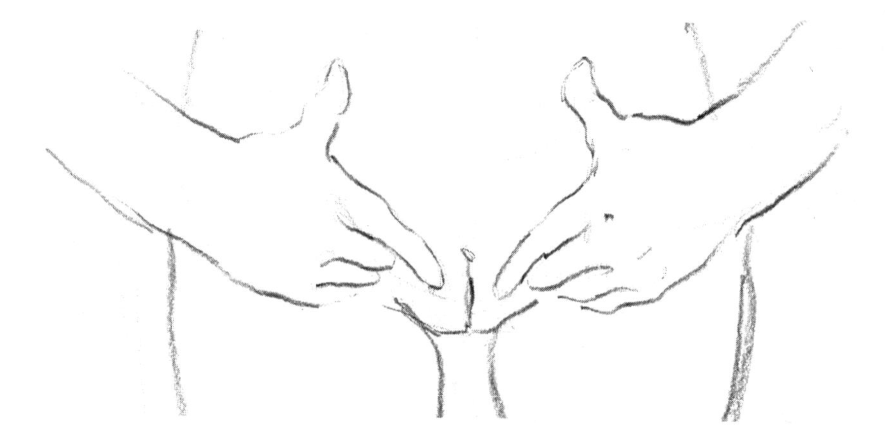

Your internal sex organs are located in your abdomen, within the area shown by the fingers.

As explained in Chapter Two, you have two kinds of sex organs: external and internal. Your external (outside) sex organs are your vaginal opening, vaginal lips (or labia), and clitoris. Your internal (inside) sex organs are your vagina, cervix, uterus, fallopian tubes, and ovaries.

Your vagina is a tube-shaped passageway that connects your outer and inner sex organs. It begins at the vaginal opening and ends inside at the cervix. Menstrual blood flows out of the vagina.

Your cervix is the opening to your uterus. In the middle of the cervix is a little hole. Menstrual blood flows out of the uterus into the vagina through this hole.

Your uterus is a muscular, baglike organ the size and shape of an upside-down pear. It is located in your lower abdomen. Babies grow in the uterus, which is also known as the womb.

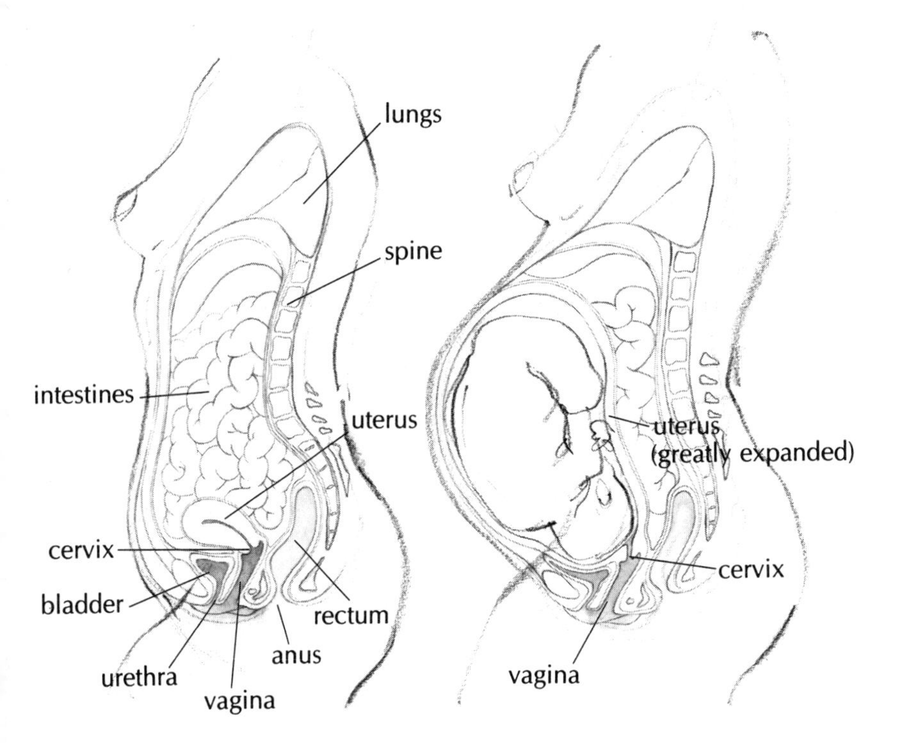

The uterus stretches to make room for a growing baby. The cervix and the vagina stretch when it's time for the baby to be born.

Your fallopian tubes are two narrow tubes connected to the uterus and extending to the ovaries.

Your ovaries are two glands, about the size and shape of almonds, located on either side of the uterus. Each ovary contains egg cells (also called "ova" [OH-vah]).

Your sex organs are regulated by two glands in your brain, the pituitary (pit-TOO-it-tare-ee) and the hypothalamus (hi-poh-THAL-ah-muss). These

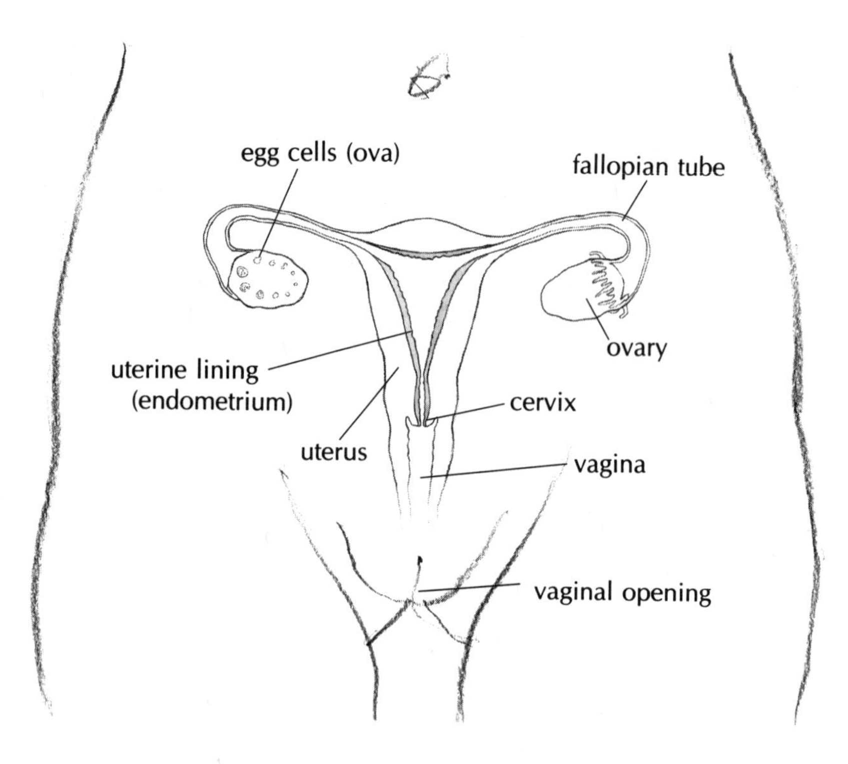

Your vagina leads to your internal sex organs.

glands, which are part of your endocrine (EN-doh-krin) system, make the hormones that control your reproductive system.

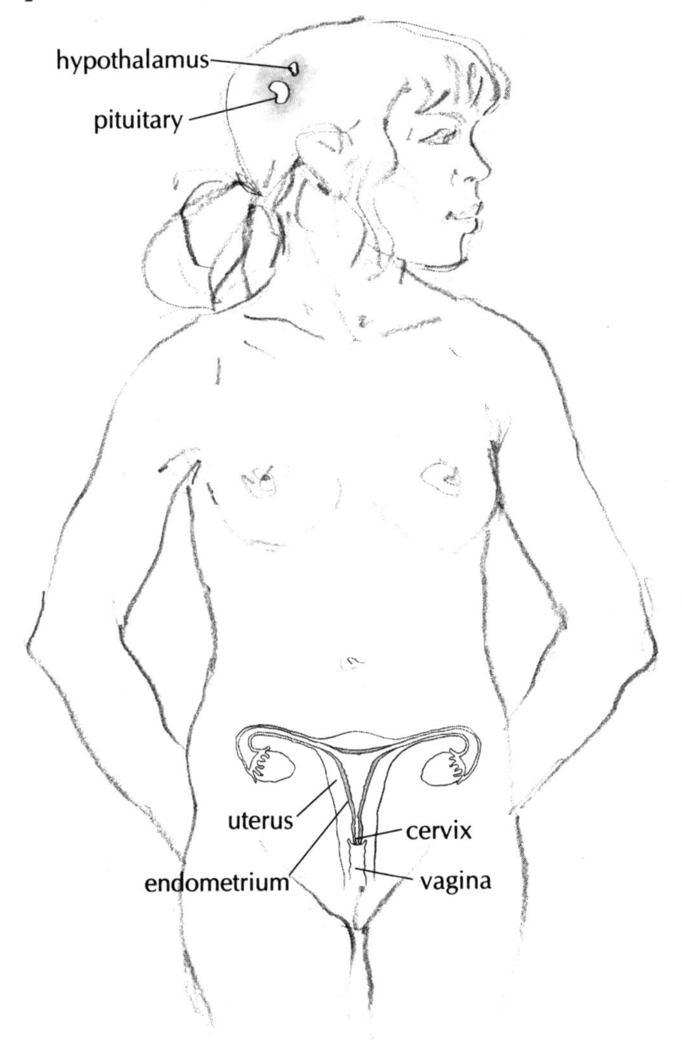

The pituitary gland in your brain controls your sex organs by sending chemical messages to them.

You know how sometimes when you say something is wrong, someone will say to you, "It's all in your head"? Now I know why they say that—because the pituitary gland *is* in my head!

Stages of the Menstrual Cycle

Each month hormones lead your body through different stages of the menstrual cycle. You may notice only the menstruating part of your cycle, but other activities are going on inside you all the time.

The cycle begins on the first day that you menstruate. Five days later, as your period is winding down or perhaps is already over, your ovaries respond to earlier hormonal signals and start ripening a number of eggs.

Your ovaries have contained about four hundred thousand egg cells, or ova, since your birth. These eggs do not develop until puberty. Then, each month, a few get ready. After they are ripe, one or more burst free from the ovary.

This egg-bursting event happens about halfway between your periods and is called "ovulation" (ah-vew-LAY-shun). Sometimes you can feel an egg ovulate inside your abdomen. It feels like a little ping, twinge, or cramp to one side of, and a bit below, your belly button. (There is a dominant ovary that ovulates most of the time.) You may also notice a mucus discharge like egg white on your underpants or when you wipe yourself. This discharge is natural; it signals ovulation. If the mucus discharge bothers you between periods, don't absorb the wetness with a tampon. Use cotton underpants, which are more absorbent than nylon, and if necessary, use a minipad or panty liner.

After ovulation the tiny (about the size of a needle point) egg, or ovum, begins an amazing journey to the uterus. First it must get to the fallopian tubes—not easy because the egg doesn't have any way to make itself move. The fallopian tube, however, is like a tiny hairy flower swaying back and forth near the ovary. The egg gets caught in the hairs and pulled into the fallopian tubes. You can't feel any of this.

The egg then travels through the fallopian tube to the uterus, a journey that takes about five days. During the journey hormones called estrogen (ESS-tra-jen) and progesterone (pro-JES-ter-own) have been causing the inside wall of your uterus to build up a fresh spongy lining soaked with blood. This is called the uterine (YOO-ter-in) lining, or endometrium (en-doh-MEE-tree-um). The purpose of the lining is to provide a soft and nourishing place in which a fertilized egg can grow into a baby.

A fertilized egg is one that has joined with a male reproductive cell (sperm) in the fallopian tube. Sperm enters the vagina during sexual in-

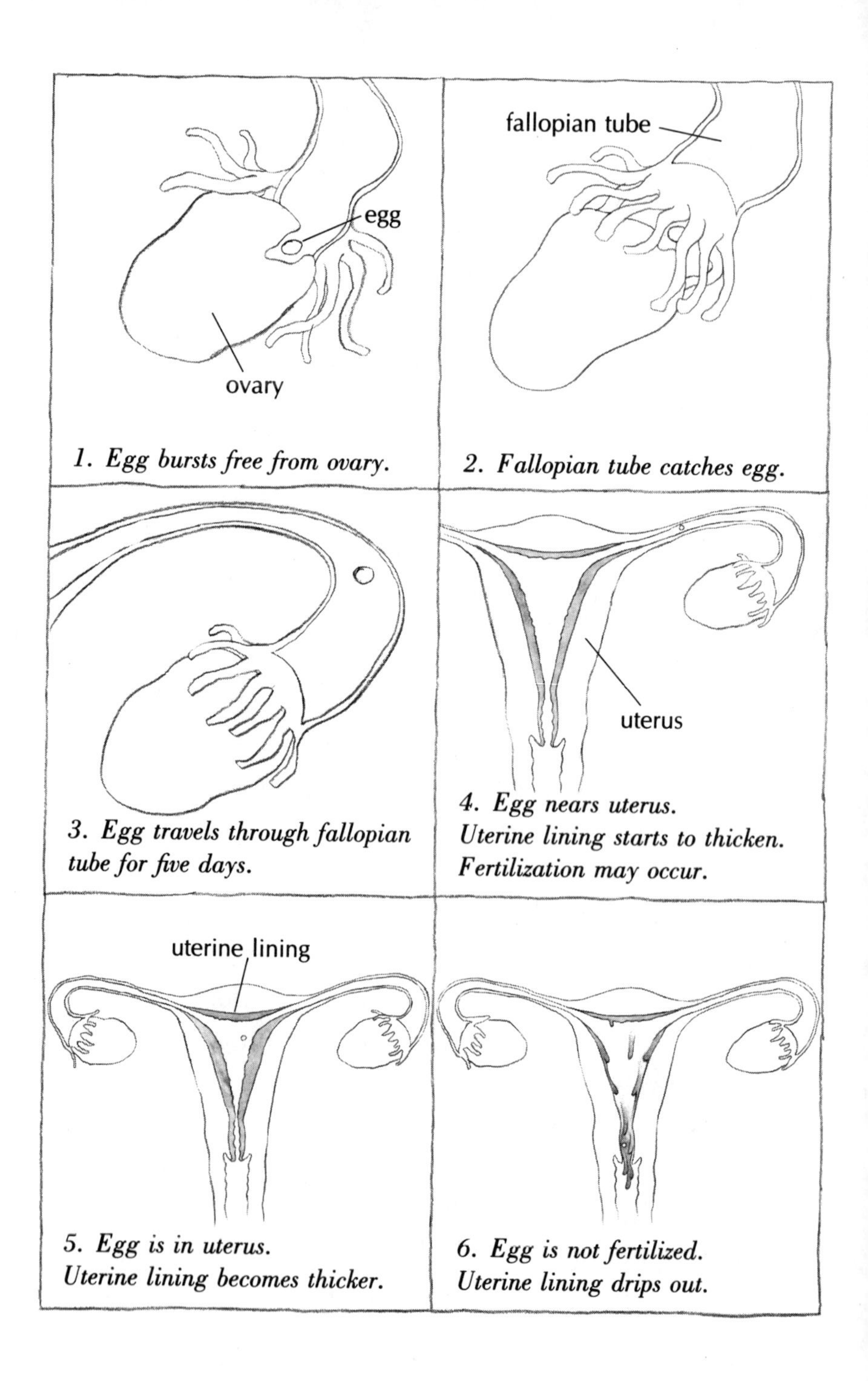
egg
ovary
1. Egg bursts free from ovary.
fallopian tube
2. Fallopian tube catches egg.
3. Egg travels through fallopian tube for five days.
uterus
4. Egg nears uterus. Uterine lining starts to thicken. Fertilization may occur.
uterine lining
5. Egg is in uterus. Uterine lining becomes thicker.
6. Egg is not fertilized. Uterine lining drips out.

tercourse, often called "making love." If the sperm and egg join together, a girl or woman becomes pregnant. For a fuller discussion of sexual intercourse and pregnancy, see pages 73–76.

If the egg is not fertilized, it does not grow into a baby. When it reaches the uterus, it dissolves. Production of estrogen and progesterone stops, and the spongy, bloody uterine lining breaks down. Menstrual blood drips out of your uterus, through your cervix, into your vagina, and then out of your body through your vaginal opening. You become aware that you are menstruating again.

By the time you have started to menstruate, hormones have told your ovary to ripen more eggs, and the menstrual cycle goes around again.

The diagram on page 38 shows the stages of the menstrual cycle. As you look at it, bear in mind that the length of any one stage can vary from girl to girl, just as the length of the cycle can vary. You can't tell how long your cycle or any of its parts are from just one time. To know your cycle well, you must observe yourself for several months and average out your experiences.

Though a diagram of the menstrual cycle may seem far removed from your actual experience of menstruation, it is a good indication of just how amazing your body is. You eat, sleep, play, go to school, talk with friends, and all the time your

The Menstrual Cycle

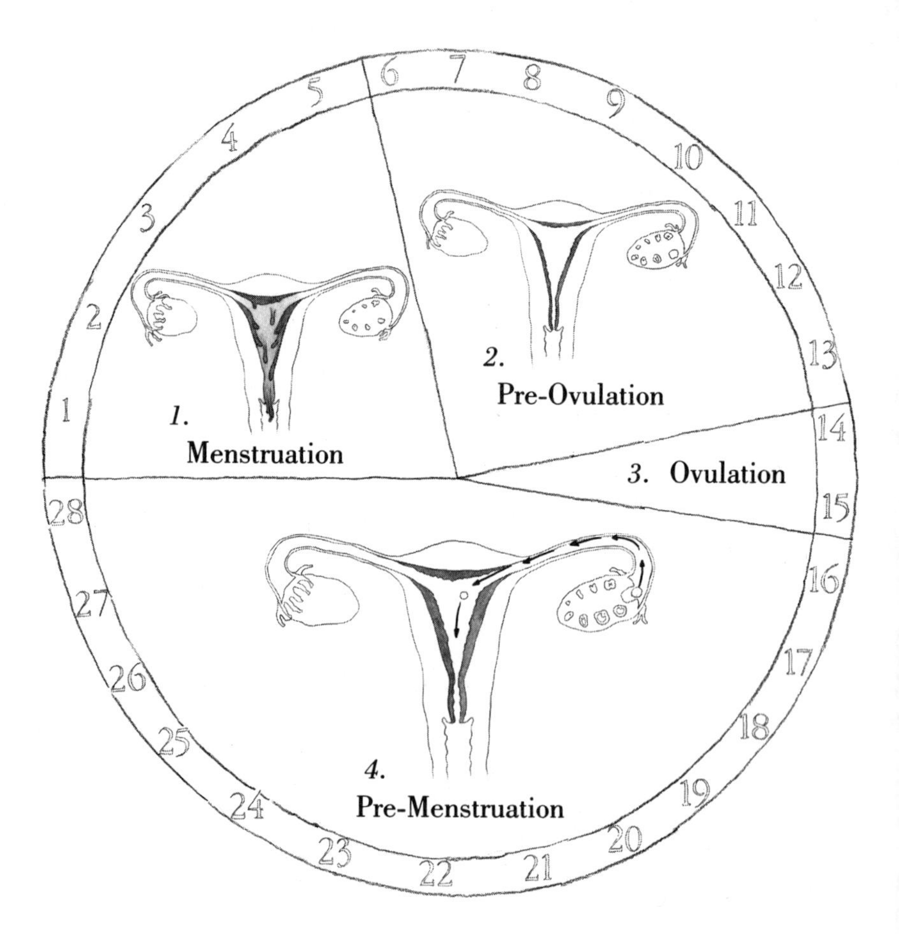

1. Uterine lining breaks down and is shed (menstruation). Bleeding lasts three to seven days.
2. Uterus has a thin lining.
3. Egg ripens and bursts free. Egg travels for five days through the fallopian tube. Lining of uterus begins to thicken.
4. Egg reaches uterus. If fertilized, egg grows into a baby in the uterus. If unfertilized, egg dissolves.

body is working in ways that you're hardly aware of: digesting food; making your muscles work; pumping blood through your limbs; breathing. One of the most amazing things your body does month after month, over and over again, is prepare to reproduce another human being. Although it is hoped that you won't use your reproductive system until you're truly ready to be a mother, knowing how amazing it is can help you gain new respect and even awe for yourself and your abilities. Such self-respect can help you in turn put menstruation into better perspective.

4 / Taking Care of Yourself During Your Period

If you look at the feminine products section in a supermarket or drugstore, you can see that there are many different products for taking care of yourself during your period. How much luckier we are today than our great-grandmothers were! They had to use cloths to absorb menstrual blood and had to wash them out between wearings.

The two main kinds of supplies you'll see in a store are pads (also called sanitary napkins) and tampons. The different brand names, sizes, and shapes may be confusing, so when you get a chance, take some time to read the directions and study the pictures on the packages to know what your choices are. At first you may not know whether to buy pads or tampons, or exactly how to use them, but with experience and practice you'll soon discover which products suit you. From time to time recheck the supplies on store shelves, since new products may feature improvements that you'll like.

Pads (Sanitary Napkins)

Pads absorb blood flowing out of your vagina. They come in different thicknesses to provide a range of protection. On heavy flow days and overnight you might choose a super maxipad or a night super maxi, which are about ¾″ thick. On medium flow days you might choose a regular maxipad, which is a little over ½″ thick. On a light flow day or when your period is trailing off, you might choose a minipad (about ⅜″ thick) or a panty liner (about ⅛″ thick). Panty liners are helpful for those who spot (leave a spot of blood on their underpants) and also for those who are bothered by mucus discharge when they are ovulating.

There are additional varieties of pads from which to choose. Often these varieties are explained on the boxes. Thin maxipads give you extra protection when you're too active to wear a thick maxipad comfortably. Some pads are tapered in

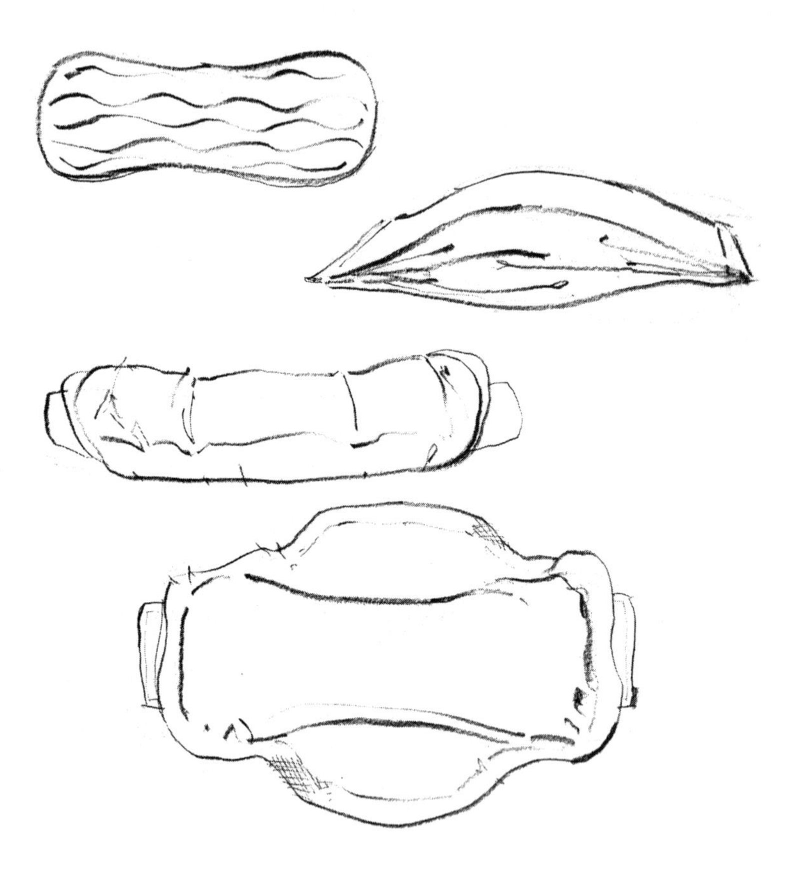

Pads come in different sizes and shapes. Find the ones you most prefer.

the middle to reduce chafing against the sides of your legs.

Most pads are beltless, which means they are kept in place by sticky strips that adhere to your panties. To wear a pad, you peel away a paper strip covering the adhesive and press the adhesive side of the pad against your panties. Your underpants should fit well and not be too loose. Some thick pads have "panty protectors," absorbent flaps that extend from the sides of the pads and fold around your underpants to keep them from getting stained on the edges and to prevent leakage onto your clothes and bedsheets. Not everyone needs such extra protection, but it can make a big difference to those who do need it.

> I wear super maxipads with panty protector wings on my heavy flow days and nights. Then I wear regular pads, and for the last few days I wear minipads.

> My period is so light, I can wear minipads the whole time.

A "tabbed" or belted pad, available in some drugstores, has long, tapered ends that fasten to special hooks on an elastic sanitary belt, which you wear around your waist. A tabbed pad doesn't have a sticky side since the sanitary belt keeps it in place. While most people use beltless pads today, some women wear belted tabbed pads out of habit—belted pads used to be the only kind of pads on the market—and because they like the way the belt holds the pads close to the body.

Deodorant pads are scented with fragrance intended to cover up embarrassing odors. Such perfumes are not necessary and may even be irritating (if you experience irritation, switch to unscented pads). Unpleasant menstrual odors are caused by damp blood that has been on a pad for more than four hours. As the blood combines with oxygen, it can have an odor. To keep your scent fresh, bathe daily and change your pads every one to four hours. If you feel that you need to wash your pubic area during the day, you can use personal towelettes that come in little foil packages. Use only the towelettes that are made for feminine hygiene; these are mild enough not to irritate your vaginal tissues. Wipe from the front to the back, not from back to front: You don't want to spread bacteria from your anus to your vulva. If the towelettes irritate you, stop using them. A wet paper towel will work fine in an emergency.

Regardless of which pad you use, your blood should soak into the middle of it. If in changing a pad you see that your blood has soaked more toward the front or back, alter where you stick the pad onto your panties or how deeply your fasten each tab on a tabbed pad to your sanitary belt.

As your pads are used, throw them away in trash containers. A good way to discard a pad is to fold it over and roll toilet paper around it, more or less to disguise it since it is not particularly pleasant to see in the trash. Many pads come individually packaged in little plastic bags. If you save the bag in your purse or pocket, you can use it to discard the pad when you're done with it.

In most public rest rooms there are convenient containers on the sides of stalls for the disposing of pads. Do not throw pads down the toilet—they are too big to go down. Flushed pads can cause toilets to overflow and plumbing to be damaged.

Tampons

Tampons are small sticks of absorbent materials that you insert into your vagina. A tampon soaks up menstrual blood before it drips out. When you need to change the tampon, you pull it out by a string attached to it that hangs outside your body.

Used tampons can be flushed down most toilets. However, in some homes with older plumbing tampons may get stuck in the pipes and cause toilets to overflow. If you are in doubt about flushing a tampon, roll it up in toilet paper and put it in a trash container.

There are different types and sizes of tampons. The two basic types are with and without applicators. An applicator is a plastic or cardboard tube with a plunger or little stick that holds a tampon in position and helps you to put it in your body.

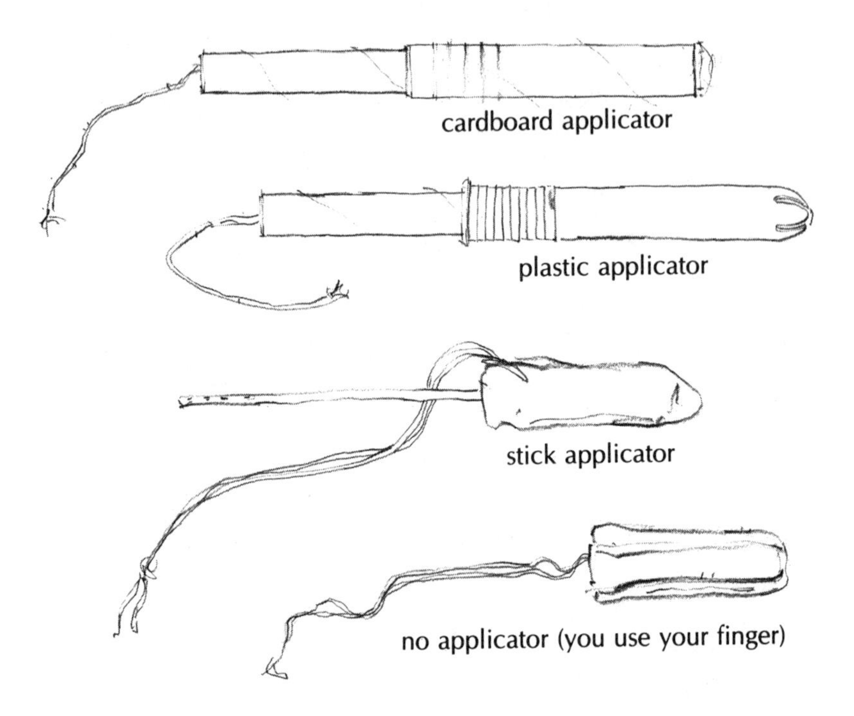

Some tampons have plastic applicators, some have cardboard applicators, some have stick applicators (less common), and some have no applicators at all.

Tampons without applicators are held and pushed in with your fingers. They are smaller than tampons with applicators, which means that since they take up less space in your pocket or purse, you can carry more of them around at a time. The advantage of tampons with applicators is that many people find them easier to insert. You might want to try both to see which you like better.

Tampons, like pads, may be scented. Such perfumes are unnecessary since there is no smell when you are wearing tampons and the perfumes can be irritating to your skin.

Tampons come in different sizes for different flows: slender for light to medium flow, regular for medium flow, super for heavy flow, and super plus for very heavy flow. If you find a tampon difficult to insert or uncomfortable to wear, try a smaller one.

HOW TO USE TAMPONS

If you are using a tampon for the first time, start with a small, thin size. Most tampons come with diagrams that show you how to use them.

While you insert a tampon it may help to picture your vagina as a collapsed four- to five-inch balloon and your vaginal opening as the opening of the balloon. You have to push the tampon past the muscles of the vaginal opening so that it stays in the vagina, not in the opening.

If you don't put the tampon in far enough, you can feel it in the opening—an uncomfortable feeling. If you put it in far enough, you won't feel it at all.

You should be able to touch the string hanging out.

> Putting in a tampon felt very awkward for the first few times. It took practice before I could do it easily.

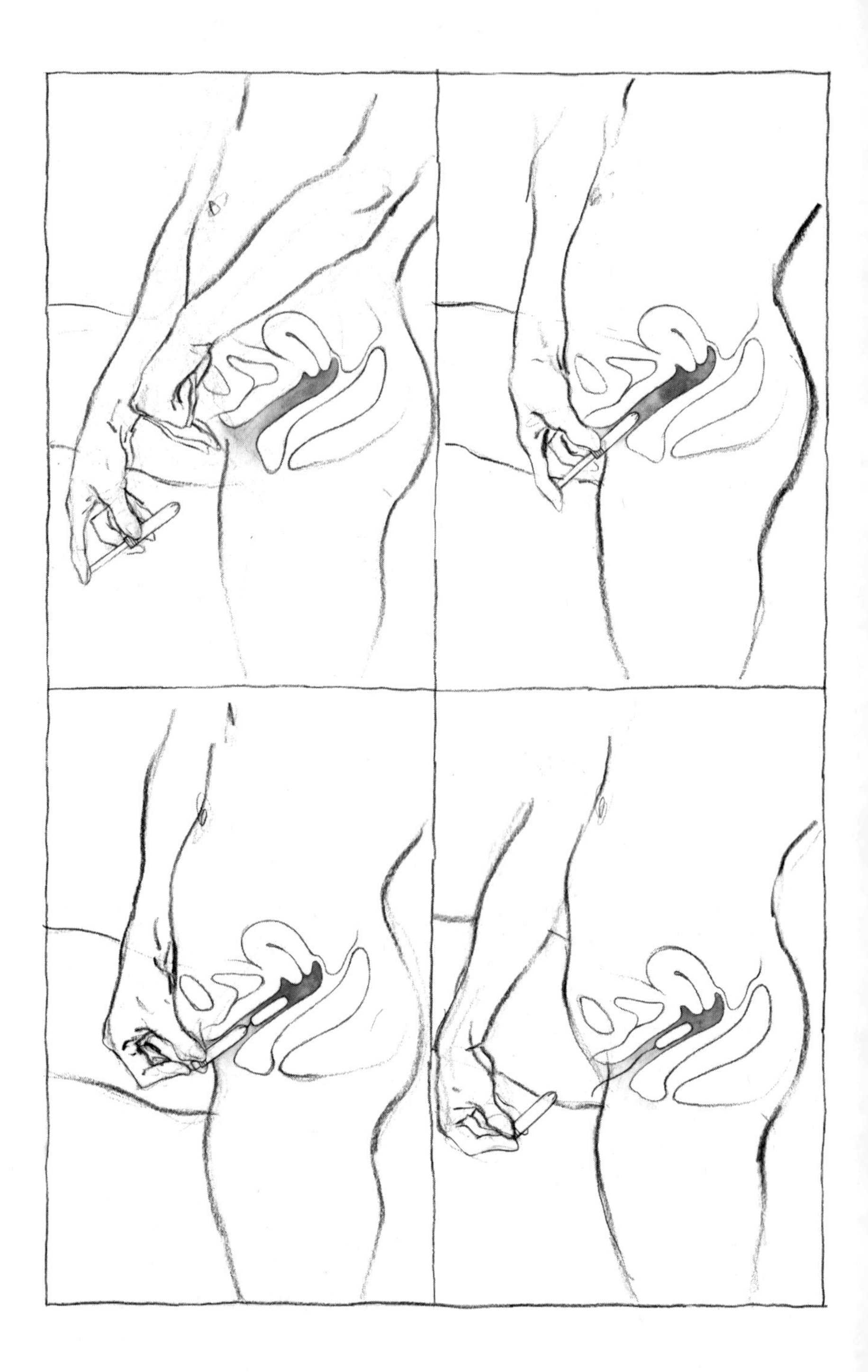

To insert a tampon with a plastic or cardboard plunger-type applicator:

1. Have clean hands. Remove the protective wrapper from the tampon. Get into a comfortable position (sitting on the toilet or standing with one foot elevated, resting on something), and relax. Take a deep breath or two to help you relax.
2. Hold the outside tube of the applicator (where the two parts of the applicator meet) between your thumb and your middle finger. Put your index finger at the end of the plunger (where the string is hanging out). With your other hand spread your vaginal lips away from your vaginal opening.
3. Place the tip of the applicator into your vaginal opening, hold it at an upward angle, and give it a gentle push toward the small of your back. Glide it in farther until the outside applicator tube is almost all the way in. You may have to maneuver the tampon a little to get it past the muscles around your vaginal opening.
4. Press the plunger (the inside part of the applicator). The plunger will expel or push the tampon into position in your vagina. Remove both parts of the applicator, which are now one inside the other, and discard. (Do not flush plastic applicators down the toilet.) The tampon should be comfortable; you shouldn't really feel it at all anymore, and its string should be hanging outside. If you still feel the tampon, you probably didn't push it up far enough. Pull it out by the string, and discard. Start fresh with a new tampon.

To insert a tampon with a stick applicator:

1. Follow the directions for the plunger-type applicator, holding the stick and the string between your fingers.
2. Push the tampon in until it's comfortably in position.
3. Let go of the string.
4. Remove the stick and throw it away in a trash container.

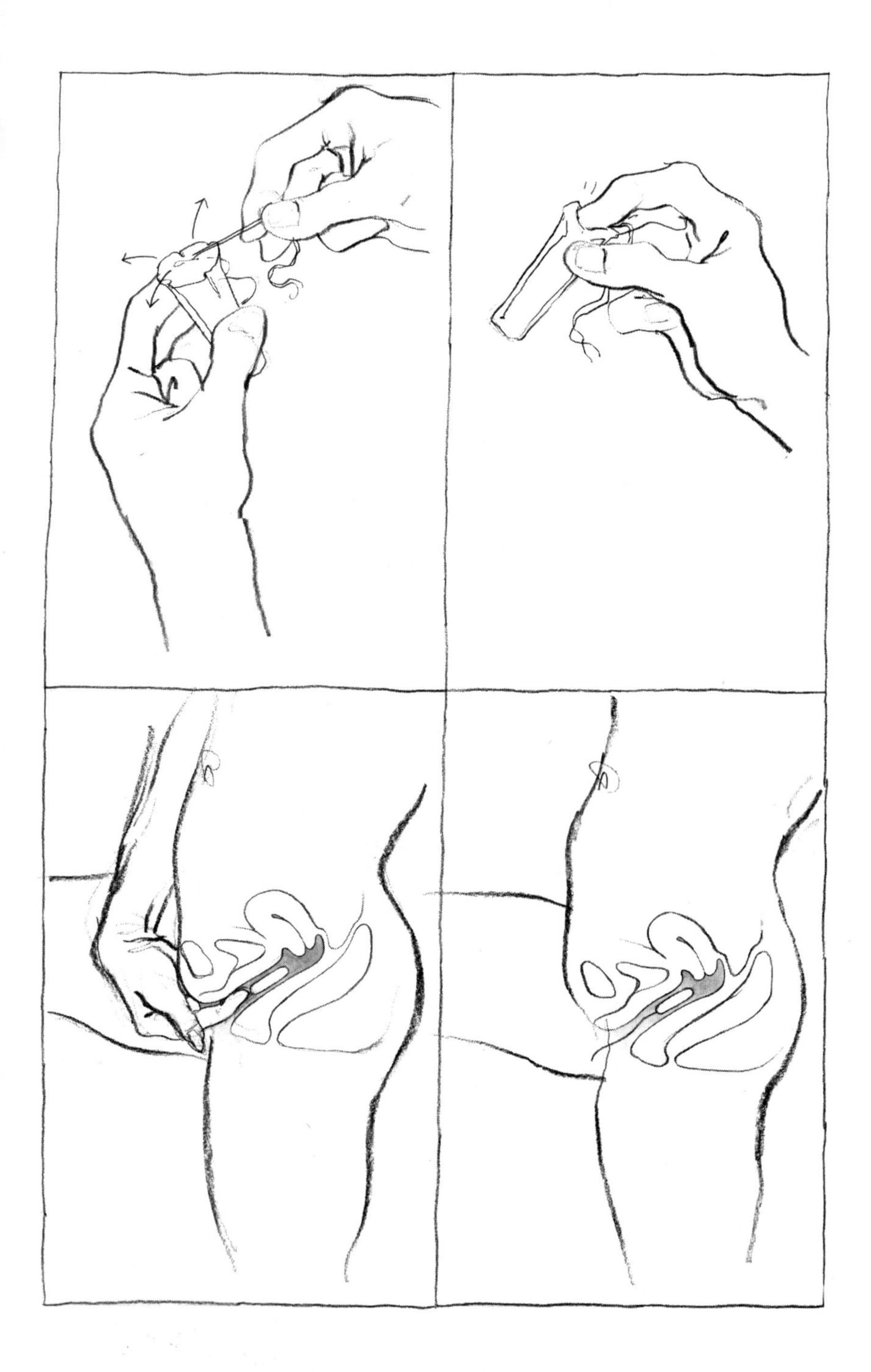

To insert a tampon without an applicator:

1. Have clean hands. Remove the protective wrapper from the tampon. Get into a comfortable position (sitting on the toilet or standing with one foot resting on something), and relax. Take a deep breath or two to help you relax.
2. Pull out the string, which is curled up at one end, and move it back and forth to widen the base of the tampon so that your finger will have a bigger and slightly indented area to push against when you insert the tampon into your body. Place your index finger in the indentation.
3. With your other hand spread your vaginal lips away from your vaginal opening.
4. Place the tampon into your vaginal opening, hold it at an upward angle, and give it a gentle push with your finger toward the small of your back. Push until the entire length of your finger is inside you. If you still feel the tampon, it hasn't gone in far enough. Relax, and push it a little farther. The tampon should come to rest inside your vagina with its string hanging outside.

COMPARING APPLICATORS

Plastic applicators have rounded ends and some people find them easier to insert than cardboard applicators. When you use one, be sure the "petals" of the round end are folded down properly before you insert the plastic applicator. A petal that is sticking up can scrape and irritate your skin.

Cardboard applicators sometimes seem dry and hard to insert. If you find this to be true, try a smaller size, which may be easier to insert, or put a little petroleum jelly (Vaseline) on the end.

Cardboard applicators and paper wrappers are biodegradable (which means that they will decompose in time after being discarded) and can be flushed down most toilets. Because plastic applicators and wrappers are *not* biodegradable, they should not be flushed away.

You also should not flush stick applicators, which are thin enough to carry in your purse or pocket until you can find a trash can.

You may want to try each kind of applicator to see which you like best.

HOW TO REMOVE A TAMPON

When you wish to remove a tampon, get into the same position you held when you inserted the tampon, and relax. Breathe deeply a few times if necessary to help you relax. Gently but firmly pull on the string at the same angle that you used to insert the tampon.

Always remove a tampon before you insert another one. Always remove the last tampon at the end of your period.

If you can't find the string, don't panic. It may be curled up in the vaginal opening or just inside the vagina. Reach up and get it with a clean finger. If you still can't get it, try squatting. It may be easier to reach that way. If you still can't reach it, don't panic. Tell someone you trust what has happened. A doctor can get the tampon out for you. This may be embarrassing, but it's not dangerous. You can't lose a tampon internally because there's no place for it to go. It is too big to pass through the cervix into the uterus.

CONCERNS ABOUT USING TAMPONS

> My mother told me not to use tampons until I was married, but she wouldn't say why.

> My mother didn't want me to use tampons, but at some point in high school friends told me that they used tampons, so I started using them too. My mother didn't object.

For various reasons some parents do not want their daughters to use tampons. One problem may be this: In a girl's vaginal opening is a thin membrane called a hymen (HI-men) and sometimes nicknamed "cherry." It used to be thought that the hymen stretched across the vagina and was broken only during sexual intercourse and that therefore, a way to determine if a girl was a virgin (someone who has never had intercourse) was for a doctor to examine the girl's hymen to see if it was intact.

Today we know that hymens vary from girl to

girl. Some stretch across the vaginal opening, and some stretch only partially across. Some hymens have holes in them, and some do not. Girls' hymens can stretch and tear from horseback riding, doing splits, falling off bikes, having intercourse, and possibly inserting tampons. When a girl's hymen is torn, it may bleed and it may not. It may hurt and it may not. The experience is different among females. Rarely does a doctor need to be called.

Some parents do not want their daughters to use tampons because they believe tampons can break hymens. Others have heard that tampons are inappropriate for young girls, but they don't know why. And still others are worried about a newly discovered risk called TSS, toxic shock syndrome.

TOXIC SHOCK SYNDROME

Tampon packages now have warnings on them that read:

> ATTENTION: Tampons are associated with Toxic Shock Syndrome (TSS). TSS is a rare but serious disease that may cause death. Read and save the enclosed information.

In 1980 researchers found an association between tampon use and a rare, but sometimes fatal, disease called toxic shock syndrome. The main symptoms of this disease are:

1. A sudden high fever (102° or more)
2. Vomiting
3. Diarrhea
4. Fainting or dizziness upon standing up
5. A rash that looks like sunburn

Other symptoms of toxic shock syndrome are aching muscles and joints, redness of the eyes, sore throat, and general weakness. If you experience any of these symptoms during your period and are wearing a tampon, remove it immediately and call a doctor. If you think you have experienced any of these symptoms before while wearing a tampon, tell your doctor about them.

To avoid the risk of TSS completely, don't use tampons. To minimize the risk, use tampons less frequently and use the smallest size possible. Although TSS is a rare disease and not always associated with tampons, six to seventeen females per hundred thousand menstruating females are estimated to get it. The rate is higher among teenage girls and women under thirty.

> To be on the safe side my mother told me to cut down on tampons. She said to use the smallest tampon that worked during the day and pads at night. She said to use minipads or panty liners on my light days.

For more information about toxic shock syndrome, read the brochures in tampon packages and consult your doctor.

Comparing Tampons and Pads

Some girls and women like pads because they are safe and in some ways easier to use for people who have trouble inserting tampons. Others like tampons because once properly inserted, they are much more comfortable than pads.

> I think tampons are easier to carry around, easier to use, and easier to dispose of than pads.

> As long as I insert them correctly, tampons are more comfortable to wear than pads.

> I like a combination of both. And not only that, I like super *and* regular tampons plus maxi *and* minipads. I keep four boxes of different supplies on hand all the time!

Many girls feel that the risk of wearing tampons is balanced by their convenience over pads. But the decision to choose tampons, pads, or both is one you will have to make, perhaps with advice from your mother or another older woman. Making thoughtful choices is another sign that you are growing up.

5 / Special Concerns

Questions and concerns about your period and puberty are to be expected because the changes you are going through are complex, involving both your physical and emotional parts. Some girls have an easier time with the physical aspects of growth; others have an easier time with the emotional aspects. Chances are you'd like to know a little bit more about both.

It is hoped that in this chapter you'll find answers to questions you may have as well as comfort in knowing that other girls your age ask the same questions you do.

What kinds of physical activity can I do during menstruation?

It used to be that women cut down on activities when they had their periods. This may have been due to the fact that the supplies they were wearing were bulky and uncomfortable. There also used to be a feeling that women were sickly when they had their periods.

Today, with better supplies and a different attitude, girls and women feel that they can do just about anything they want to do, and doctors tend to agree.

> I generally don't play sports, but if I want to while having my period, I usually do.

> I play sports and act the same as always when I have my period. At first when I used pads, sports could become uncomfortable; but about six months ago I switched to tampons, and now sports are no problem whatever.

> I play sports every season, menstruation or not.

> I wear tampons when I do sports and swim. No problem.

Doctors say that during their periods girls can take gym, swim, go horseback riding, and do gymnastics. Many girls find that they are more comfortable wearing thin maxipads or tampons when they are active.

How can I prevent a thick pad from showing through my clothing?

You can wear loose pants or skirts when you are wearing a thick pad so the pad doesn't show. You may find that skirts are more comfortable for changing supplies during the day. If you have to wear tight clothing, such as a leotard for dance class, you can use a thinner pad or a tampon.

How can I prevent my clothes from getting bloodstained?

It's a good idea to wear dark clothes and prints on your menstrual days to save yourself from embarrassment should blood stain your clothes. If you think you might get your period, it might be better to play it safe and not wear white or light slacks on the day you are expecting it. Or make sure you have a long jacket or sweater handy to use for a cover-up. For extra protection against staining, wear a pad with panty protector flaps.

What should I do if my clothes get stained?

If you are in a place where you can conveniently wash the spot, do it as soon as you can, preferably while the stain is still red. Blood turns brown with exposure to air and becomes harder to remove. Use cold water with soap or detergent. If there's no soap, just use cold water.

If you can't do anything about the stain, hope that people won't notice it and try to forget about it until you get home. This is more easily done in a large, crowded department store than at school! If you have stained noticeably at school, share your problem with a sympathetic teacher. Perhaps the teacher will give you time to go to the bathroom to wash the spot. Maybe the teacher, principal, or nurse will let you rest in a private office until the wet spot dries, if it is very noticeable. Again, you might want to keep a long sweater or jacket at school in case of spotting emergencies.

What should I do if I get my period somewhere and don't have supplies with me?

Sometimes you can buy a tampon or pad from a dispenser in a girls' room. Or you can just call out from your stall, "Does anyone have a spare tampon? I just got my period and I don't have any." Thank the person who helps you.

If nothing is available, put some toilet paper in your panties and go without protection for a short while until you can go to the nurse's office or a store to get a pad or tampon. Most women and girls are helpful in such situations because they experience them too. If you need to borrow money to buy supplies, don't be embarrassed to ask.

If you are at home and can't get to a store, fold up a clean washcloth or handkerchief or perhaps another pair of underpants, and place them in your panties.

To prevent this problem from occurring, carry around some supplies with you on the days you are expecting your period.

My pad scrapes the skin between my legs. What should I do?

Try changing the size or brand of your pad. Some pads are tapered in the middle to reduce this problem. Changing your pads more often may help too. Tampons do not cause chafing.

Sometimes I get pimples just before my period. What can I do about them?

Some girls find that they get a pimple or two just before their periods. If you do get a pimple, put a little acne cream on it and try to forget about it. Don't pick pimples; keep them clean and eventually they will go away. If you have a consistent or serious problem, seek help from a dermatologist (skin doctor).

What can I do about cramps?

Some girls get cramps, or muscular aches, in their stomach area when they have their periods, especially on the first day. Many girls do not get them.

> I have terrible cramps. They last about six hours, and all that helps is to lie down with a heating pad on my abdomen. I also take Midol.

> My cramps last for two days, but they're not really painful, just uncomfortable.

> My worst problem is cramps. No exercises help; they just make it worse. My only solution is to grimace and bear it.

> I get bad cramps in my lower back. I usually take aspirin, and that helps somewhat.

> I didn't get cramps the first ten times, but they did start only a little while ago. They are just uncomfortable, nothing to send me to bed.

If you don't have cramps, don't wish you did or invent them to be like someone else. It's not worth it. If you do have them, you have your choice of various kinds of relief.

One kind of relief may come from not dwelling on the cramps too much. Worrying about them may cause you to imagine that they are worse than they really are. Often as girls grow older, their cramps lessen or go away altogether.

Good diet, enough water, sufficient sleep, and plenty of exercise will keep your body healthy and less susceptible to cramps. Eating foods that cause you to have regular bowel movements may relieve cramps. Incidentally, your bowels may be runny and soft at the beginning of your period—nature's way of relieving pressure on your uterus that may make you uncomfortable. You may find that standing straighter so that you have better posture will take pressure off your uterus and thus relieve your cramps.

Daily exercises, such as the following ones that improve posture and muscle tone, may prevent cramps.

Touch Your Toes

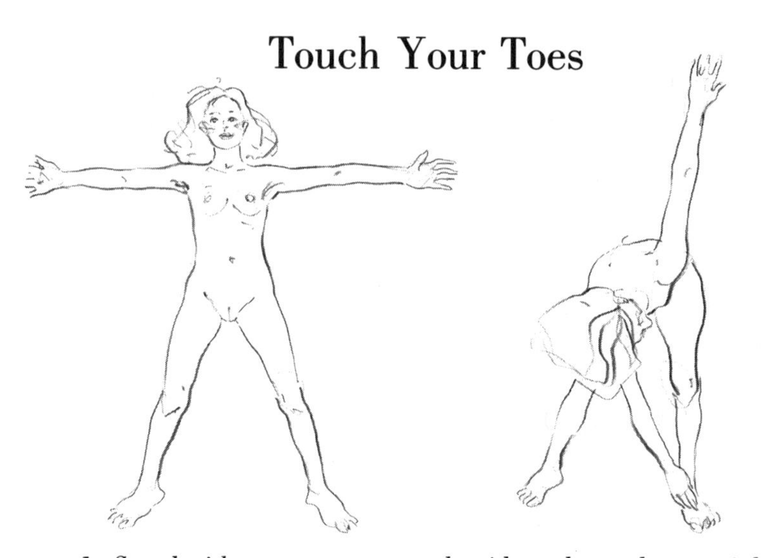

1. Stand with your arms out to the side and your legs straight. 2. Twist at the waist and bend, touching your right hand to your left foot. Straighten. Repeat four times. 3. Switch sides, touching your left hand to your right foot. Repeat four times.

Stretch to the Sky

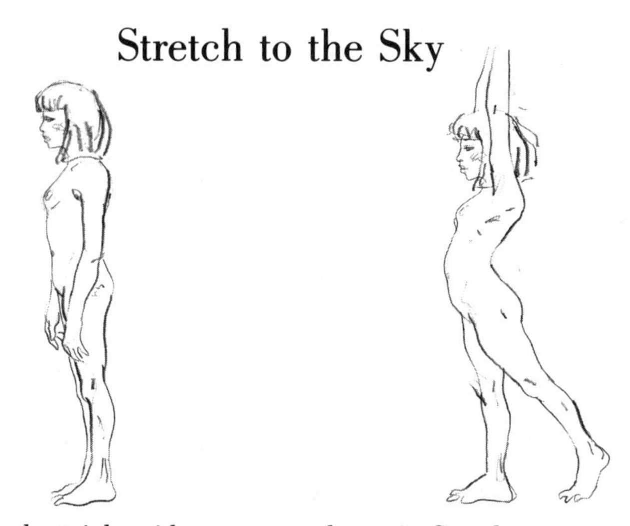

1. Stand straight with your arms down. 2. Stretch your arms up to the sky; at the same time stretch your left leg backward. Repeat four times. 3. Switch sides, stretching your right leg backward. Repeat four times.

You can obtain relief from cramps through a combination of heat and mental relaxation. Take a warm, unhurried bath to soothe your muscles, or lie down with a hot-water bottle or heating pad on your stomach. Meditate about calming things, making sure you are breathing in a restful way.

If you have bad cramps at school, ask whether you may lie down in the nurse's office for a while. The nurse may have a heating pad or hot-water bottle you can use.

You may also obtain relief from cramps through medication. Look in your drugstore or supermarket for an over-the-counter (nonprescription) medication that relieves menstrual cramps. There are a number of such products, including Midol, Tylenol, Nuprin, Advil, and other brand names. If the cramps are severe, do *not* increase the dosage of medication. Instead consult with your doctor and ask for a prescription medication. Don't be afraid to explain about your cramps. Doctors, nurses, and pharmacists are used to such problems.

Why do I feel bloated before my period? Why do my breasts swell up and feel tender? What can I do about these uncomfortable feelings?

Before your period you may feel bloated and actually gain a little more weight as the result of water retention. Water retention means that throughout your body your tissues are absorbing or retaining extra water. (This water retention may cause you to feel fat and sometimes to have painful breasts. Plan to wear loose, comfortable clothes and perhaps a looser bra at the start of your period.) After you have menstruated, the water is released; you lose its weight, and your breasts are no longer swollen or achy.

One important way to reduce the discomfort is to avoid salty foods before your period. Many foods (especially potato chips and other snacks, as well as cold cuts, fast foods, and some diet sodas) are high in salt. Salt retains water, so cutting back on salty foods can help relieve your body's water retention.

It's also a good idea to stay away from caffeine—found in cola drinks, coffee, tea, and chocolate—since it too can worsen breast swelling and tenderness.

If water retention continues to be a problem, however, consult a doctor.

Why do I feel crabby, moody, or sad before my period?

Some girls and women feel tense and anxious for a day or two or even several days before their periods. This feeling is one of several symptoms that characterize a disorder known as PMS, or premenstrual syndrome. Some people with mild forms of PMS experience easily hurt feelings, tearfulness, and feelings of frustration. Normal everyday problems plus water retention plus heightened emotions caused by hormonal changes may make life seem very difficult.

If you experience such sensitivity (and not everyone does), try to understand that your period may be coming, and give yourself and others extra tolerance. Charting your periods on a monthly calendar will help you see when they are coming and help you understand better why you may be more emotional at certain times than at others.

By getting enough sleep, drinking enough water, and by avoiding foods high in salt, sugar, or caffeine before your period, you can help your body to cope better with water retention, stress, and the hormonal changes of menstruation.

A small percentage of girls, however, experience serious physical and emotional strain in the days before their periods. These symptoms of severe PMS may include depression, migraine headaches, or extreme mood swings and are clearly linked to the time before menstruation. It's important to get medical help for severe PMS.

What can I do to cope with my heaviest days of bleeding?

Wear a super tampon together with a maxipad, perhaps one with panty protector flaps. If this arrangement is insufficient, try a super plus tampon instead of a super tampon.

Change your tampon and/or pad frequently. If you feel your pad or tampon becoming full, don't take a chance. Change it. If you are busy with someone and feel blood running over, excuse yourself to go to the bathroom. Just say, "Excuse me, I'll be right back."

Make sure that on your heavy days you have enough extra supplies with you. Fill a plastic makeup bag with supplies and keep it in your purse or school bag. If you have to take it to the bathroom at school, you won't look too conspicuous.

Tampons may be carried in your purse, pocket, or book bag. Tampons without applicators are smaller than those with applicators, allowing you to carry several in a pocket at one time, if you have to. Some pads come folded in individual wrappers, which fit into your purse or a big pocket.

If you need to, you can use the wrapper to store a used pad until you can dispose of it.

If you have severe or persistent problems with heavy bleeding or cramps, consult a gynecologist.

What is a gynecologist?

A gynecologist (often called a "G.Y.N.," the abbreviation of the word *gynecologist*) is a doctor specializing in the female sex organs. Often a gynecologist is also an obstetrician ("O.B."), a doctor who specializes in pregnancy and birth.

You don't have to visit a gynecologist when you begin to menstruate because usually menstruation occurs naturally and in a healthy way; medical advice is not necessary. However, some gynecologists like to see young girls to teach them about menstruation and other aspects of puberty. Your doctor may have special reading materials for you.

What happens if my periods are late, irregular, or not coming at all?

Late, irregular, or absent periods occur for a variety of reasons.

First of all, during your first couple of years of menstruating, your periods may be irregular because it may take time for your body to establish a predictable pattern.

> I got my period ten months ago, and it's been irregular ever since.

> My periods are pretty regular now, although sometimes they come late.

> I'm not really regular because my body doesn't have a strong pattern down pat yet.

> I always get my periods twenty-six to twenty-seven days apart, like clockwork.

> My periods are now very irregular and come at completely unexpected and often inconvenient times. I always have tampons in my purse, just in case.

Secondly, even after you have established a predictable pattern, your cycle may be disrupted. If you follow both a very strict diet and a very strenuous exercise regimen, your periods may stop. This sometimes happens to professional dancers, runners, and high-level gymnasts. Runners, for example, who run twenty-five to fifty miles a week may stop menstruating.

One explanation for this phenomenon is that if you lose weight below a certain point, your body reacts as if you were in danger of starving. It shuts down your reproductive hormones as if to say that you are in no shape to make a baby. To get your reproductive system going again, you need to gain body fat. A certain amount of body fat is necessary for good health. Between seventeen and twenty-two percent of your total weight must be body fat in order for your reproductive system to function normally. If you are a very active, very thin athlete who is not menstruating, you may find that gaining some weight will get your periods going again. You may want to talk about these concerns with your doctor, coach, or dance instructor.

A low-weight/high-exercise regimen may not only cause some girls and women to stop having periods, but may also delay some thin young athletes from getting their first periods. These girls may need only a slight weight gain to start the process of puberty.

Thirdly, certain drugs, such as tranquilizers, and certain medical problems, such as an ovarian cyst (a saclike growth in an ovary) or diabetes, may stop you from getting your period.

Fourthly, strong emotions brought on by special events, such as a highly competitive track meet, going to camp, or the illness of a loved one, may make a period late. Simply worrying about your period may make it a few days late.

Fifthly, if you are pregnant, you usually will not menstruate. (Some women have a very light period during the first month.)

How do I get pregnant?

The way you get pregnant is by having sexual intercourse, often called "making love." During sexual intercourse a male puts his erect or stiff penis into your vagina. Sperm (male cells) shoot out of his penis in a creamy white liquid called "semen" (SEE-men) or "come" in an act called "ejaculation" (ee-jack-yoo-LAY-shun) or "coming."

During intercourse between three hundred million and five hundred million microscopic sperm cells are ejaculated into the vagina. These sperm can swim up the vagina, through the cervix, into the uterus, and down the fallopian tubes. In order to make a baby, an egg and a sperm have to join. This is usually done in the fallopian tubes. From there the fertilized egg travels to the uterus, where it settles into the soft uterine lining and grows into a baby. The uterine lining nourishes and supports the baby.

If pregnancy begins, the uterine lining is not shed, and menstruation does not take place. Not getting her period on time is one of the first indications to a woman that she may be pregnant. A girl who thinks she's pregnant should tell someone who can help her. This person could be a relative, friend, teacher, guidance counselor, member of the clergy (priest, minister, or rabbi), or counselor at Planned Parenthood or other family planning clinic.

In learning about your cycle, notice that menstruation and ovulation occur about two weeks apart from each other. When you are older, it will help to know that ovulation, the time halfway between your periods (twelve to fifteen days before you start menstruating), is the time that you are most fertile ("fertile" means "able to get pregnant").

Some women think that there are "safe" times during their cycles when they can have sex and yet avoid pregnancy, but this is incorrect. Cycles can be irregular; ovulation can occur at unusual times; sperm can live in the vagina for twenty-four hours. All these factors mean that women can get pregnant at *any* time during the month.

Why do I need to know about pregnancy now?

Girls and boys often pick up incorrect information about sex from each other, or they get the wrong ideas from movies and books. Young people need to learn correct information. Many teenage pregnancies today are caused by girls and boys not knowing or misunderstanding the simple facts of life.

What should I know about AIDS and other sexually transmitted diseases?

Sexually transmitted diseases (STDs), such as gonorrhea, syphilis, herpes, hepatitis B, and venereal warts, are diseases that can be spread from one person to another through sexual activity. You may learn about the acquisition, symptoms, and treatment of these diseases from your teachers, school nurse, doctor, and parents. Should you have any questions about these diseases now, ask an adult whom you trust to help you with correct information.

The most important sexually transmitted disease for you to know about is AIDS (Acquired Immune Deficiency Syndrome) because AIDS is fatal, which means it eventually causes death, and because thus far there is no cure for AIDS, though certain medicines can bring some relief. The AIDS virus (called the HIV virus) lives in body fluids—blood, semen, vaginal fluids and, in very small amounts, saliva and tears. AIDS is not spread from one person to another easily. You can't catch it from touching, hugging, or being coughed at or sneezed upon by a person infected with AIDS.

To catch AIDS the AIDS virus must get from the body fluids of an infected person into your bloodstream. The two main ways this happens are through sexual intercourse and intravenous (I.V.) drug use. (AIDS also can be spread by blood transfusions, but this danger has diminished as hospitals now routinely check their blood supply for the AIDS virus. In addition, a pregnant woman with AIDS can transmit the disease to her baby.)

If you avoid sexual intercourse until you're older and mature enough to enjoy it safely with a responsible person, and if you don't ever shoot drugs, you are unlikely to get AIDS. If you have a question about AIDS, ask your teacher, school nurse, doctor, or parents; or call your local AIDS hotline. Ask your telephone operator for the number. If you can't get the number, call 1-800-342-AIDS.

When should I see a doctor or gynecologist?

If you have a problem with menstruation, such as irregular periods, absent periods, painful periods, bleeding between periods, or burning vaginal discharges, let your pediatrician, family doctor, school nurse, or gynecologist know. If you don't have a gynecologist, other health practitioners can refer you to one. It may be a good idea to see your gynecologist for a yearly checkup.

If you don't have problems with menstruation, you can wait to see a gynecologist until you're eighteen or so—then schedule a gynecological checkup every year.

What is it like to go to a gynecologist?

In the waiting room you are likely to be asked to fill out a form that includes your name, address, medical problem (if you have one), and the date of your last menstrual period. It's good to think about that date ahead of time so you can remember.

Sometimes you'll be asked to give a specimen, an inch or so of urine in a plastic cup. The nurse will give you the cup. Usually you leave it in the bathroom after you are finished, with a label or slip of paper identifying it as yours. The urine specimen is used to test for infections or sugar in your urine that may mean you are diabetic. If your doctor has time, he or she might show you how the tests are done. Don't be afraid to ask questions; most doctors like to explain things to young people. If your doctor doesn't like to do so, you might consider getting one who's more friendly and helpful.

You'll be asked to undress privately and put on

a gown like a short nightgown (it may be made of paper). In the examination room the doctor may feel your breasts to see if there are any unusual lumps. Though this may be awkward for you, it is part of the doctor's job, and he or she is quite used to it. If you like, ask your mother or an older friend to stay with you.

Doctors see girls with all sorts of bodies. Don't feel shy about yours; it is not skinnier or fatter or more beautiful or less beautiful than other bodies they've seen. Besides, doctors don't look at your body that way. They don't judge you, so try to feel relaxed. The more comfortable you are, the better you will feel.

An internal, or pelvic, exam may take place if the doctor thinks it's necessary. Again, although this procedure is definitely not routine for you, it is for the doctor. During an internal exam you will be asked to lie back on an examination table and rest your feet in "stirrups" or footholds at the end of the table. To examine your vagina your doctor puts one or two gloved fingers in the vagina with the other hand on your abdomen. The procedure, which enables your doctor to check your internal organs, may feel uncomfortable, but it takes only a few moments and it is routine.

Afterward you dress privately and often go to the doctor's office to talk with him or her. (You

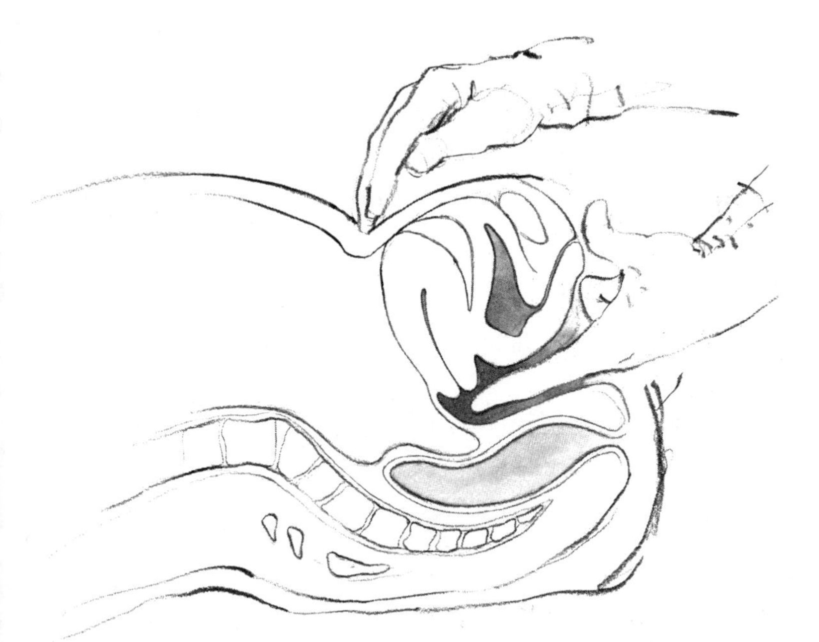

A pelvic, or internal, exam allows a doctor to check your internal organs.

may have talked with the doctor before the exam too.) In the waiting room, examining room, and doctor's office you may be asked questions about your periods: when your last one was, how often you have them, how long they last, whether they are regular, and so forth. Tell the nurse or doctor the truth without embarrassment. Don't change the information to make it sound better or worse. Your doctor needs correct information to help you be healthy. Sometimes girls, out of awkwardness, say they don't know the answers to such questions. If you're shy, it may help to tell the doctor that you feel nervous but that you will answer questions anyway. You should feel proud that you are grown-up enough to know and talk about your own menstrual experience.

What is menopause?

When you get to be about forty-five to fifty-five years old, you will stop menstruating. This change, called "menopause" or "change of life," is more or less the opposite natural process of what you are going through during puberty. Like puberty, menopause is a series of hormonally caused changes that take place over a period of time. The main event of menopause is the end of menstruation, which usually follows a period of menstrual irregularity. After menopause a woman can no longer get pregnant. During menopause women may feel the same things you do: excitement, confusion, anxiety, and the need to take time to adjust. Often they too will visit gynecologists to ask questions and seek advice.

What if I have other questions that aren't answered in this book?

If you have questions about yourself that are not answered in this book, ask someone you trust to answer them: your mother, father, grandmother, aunt, older sister, teacher, school nurse, doctor, gym teacher, family planning counselor, childbirth instructor, or religious counselor. Perhaps you have a pediatrician with whom you would feel comfortable talking. Many people are qualified to answer your questions; take the responsibility to find one you like and trust. Your library may have other books on the subject that will interest you.

6 / Other People and How They See You

Although most people will not know that you've started menstruating, some of your close friends will know about it because you'll tell them, and most of your family will know about it because families usually do. Even people you might like to keep your secrets from will know you are going through puberty because of changes in the shape of your body. Thus, at this time of your life your relationships with friends and family members may change a little.

Girlfriends

Girlfriends who have already started their periods may feel close to you, and you may feel the same way about them. You might compare your periods with them, sharing problems and ways to cope. Being able to talk together about life changes may make a friendship stronger.

> My friend Donna was the only one who really understood how bad my cramps were. My mother and the school nurse always told me I'd feel better soon. They didn't realize what agony I was in.

If you begin to menstruate before other girls that you know, you may have mixed feelings. One part of you may feel more grown-up, another may feel uncertain about the new change.

> I had two different groups of girlfriends in fifth grade. One developed early like me, and the other didn't. When I got my period, I started hanging around with the girls who were developed because I felt more comfortable talking to those who knew from their own experience the new kinds of feelings I was having.

On the other hand, if some girls get their periods before you do, you may wonder how long you have to wait, and you may feel a little left out.

However you cope with unfamiliar feelings, it's important to show your maturity in a positive, supportive way. Unfortunately, there are people who can be difficult.

> My next-door neighbor started to tease me when I grew breasts. "Booby-booby-booby" she'd say in the cafeteria, and then she and her friends would crack up. We'd been good friends before that.

If people tease you, ignore them, or if you think they can understand, ask them to stop. If the teasing persists, tell a grown-up who will help you.

The main point is that girls can be sensitive to each other's problems and needs—no matter how old they are when puberty begins.

Your Mother and Other Female Relatives

Menstruating may make you feel closer to your mother or to another woman friend or relative who is especially important to you. This person can help you buy supplies and may be there to talk to you about things like whether or not to use tampons, what to do for cramps, and how to wash out stains.

Some mothers enjoy sharing information about menstruation and biology with their daughters. They look forward to the day when their daughters get their periods, and they are justifiably proud of them. Some have planned ahead of time what to say and do to celebrate.

> My mother was thrilled. I couldn't believe how excited she got when I told her I had started menstruating.

> My aunt had told me all about it before it happened. She told me that she'd take me out to dinner when it happened, and she did.

On the other hand, some mothers are quite shy about menstruation. If they could avoid discussing it, they would. Such mothers may feel embarrassed to discuss the subject even with their own doctors and friends. When these mothers are confronted with their daughters' getting their periods for the first time, they don't know what to do, and they don't know how to explain the menstrual cycle scientifically.

> My mother acted strange, almost unfriendly. I finally realized that she was embarrassed and didn't quite know what to say.

> My stepmother wanted to talk with me all about it, but she seemed unhappy about something.

Sometimes a mother feels surprised and even a little sad that her "little girl" has started menstruating. She may feel old and afraid that her child will grow up and leave. Of course, the facts are that mothers *are* older than their children and that their children *will* grow up and have lives of their own, but these facts of life may be a little hard to take sometimes.

If you feel your mother is a little sad about your growing up, try to be understanding. Your mother will probably get over her sad and surprised feelings quickly, and then the two of you may feel closer than ever.

Your Father and Other Male Relatives

> Once my mother asked my father *right in front of me* to drive to the store for sanitary napkins. I ran upstairs and burst into tears, I was so embarrassed.

Not all girls are embarrassed about menstrual matters in front of their fathers or other male relatives. Some may tell their fathers outright that they got their periods while others will expect their mothers to do so.

Like your mother, your father may feel a little surprised that you are growing up, but he too will come to accept your changing body. It is, of course, difficult for fathers to know exactly what you are going through. Though men can read and talk about menstruating, they cannot do it. It is, along with giving birth, something only women do. Men often feel mystified about these processes and as a result may prefer not to say too much about them.

Still, not all men are alike, and some girls, for example, those who live with their fathers and not their mothers, can discuss such matters with their fathers. These fathers usually have thought about their daughters' first periods ahead of time and may have asked female friends, relatives, doctors, nurses, or teachers to help explain.

Your Sisters

Older sisters may be pleased that you have started menstruating. The change makes you less of a "kid sister" and more of an equal. Older sisters can give help and advice to you and your friends too.

On the other hand, an older sister who's jealous of you may not like to see you become more of an equal. She may be unhappy about your being "grown-up" too.

Younger sisters may be curious to know what's going on, and if you don't act too superior, they may let you tell them. On the other hand, they may not want to know. All your efforts to share information with a younger sister may be spurned with a "Yuk-I-couldn't-care-less-that's-not-going-to-happen-to-me-ever" attitude.

Your Brothers

Brothers may be curious about your menstruation. Again, remember it is something they cannot ever experience. They may ask questions or want to see a tampon or sanitary pad. They may have seen ads on TV that they don't quite understand. While they may feel free to ask you about the topic, they are more likely to feel shy. In their embarrassment they may tease you or even spy on you.

You have a right to privacy. If your brother invades your privacy, speak to him about it. If necessary, ask a parent to help you enforce your rights. A good way to cope with teasing is to ignore it. If you don't give a teaser the satisfaction of annoying you, he'll soon go away.

Keep in mind that your brother, like other members of your family, is reacting to the change in you. Instinctively he realizes that you are different in a special way. But sometimes brothers are not aware of what you are going through.

> The only person who makes my menstrual problems worse is my brother, who does so unconsciously by hogging the bathroom for a long time so I can't get at the maxipads.

If your brother doesn't seem to understand your special needs at certain times of the month, ask a parent or friend to explain the situation to him. You may want to be part of the discussion, but you don't have to be. And, of course, you could always move the supplies to your room to avoid that particular conflict.

Boys Your Own Age

Like your brothers, boys your own age will be curious about menstruation. These boys, some of whom you may have known for a long time and have been good friends with, may begin to act differently toward you. Sometimes they may act as if they hated girls, as if they were looking for ways to torment you. They may start laughing more about body parts, such as breasts and penises, and body functions, such as urinating and passing gas.

Both girls and boys go through puberty. Girls usually go through it ahead of boys; that is why they are often taller than boys. In both sexes it is the pituitary gland that gets puberty going, but the outcome for boys is different from that for girls.

Boys do not produce eggs and menstrual blood. Their role in the reproductive process is to provide sperm. Sperm are male reproductive cells. To make a baby, a sperm from the male has to fertilize an egg from the female.

During puberty boys change in a number of ways: They grow pubic hair, facial hair, and underarm hair. Sweat glands start to function, causing body odor, and facial skin and hair become oilier—changes necessitating daily bathing and perhaps a deodorant. Boys grow taller and heavier, and their penises grow larger and darker. Their voices get lower. Clefts or divisions form in their chests, and their shoulders broaden.

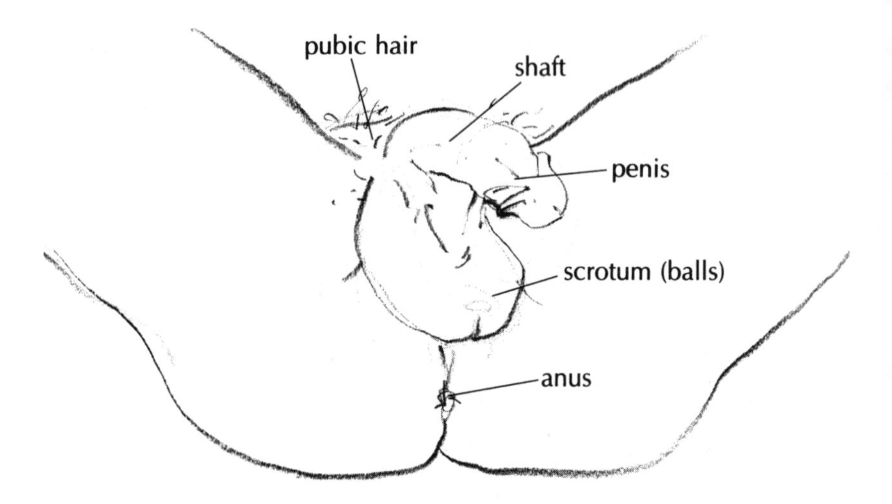

Male Genitals

How Boys Change

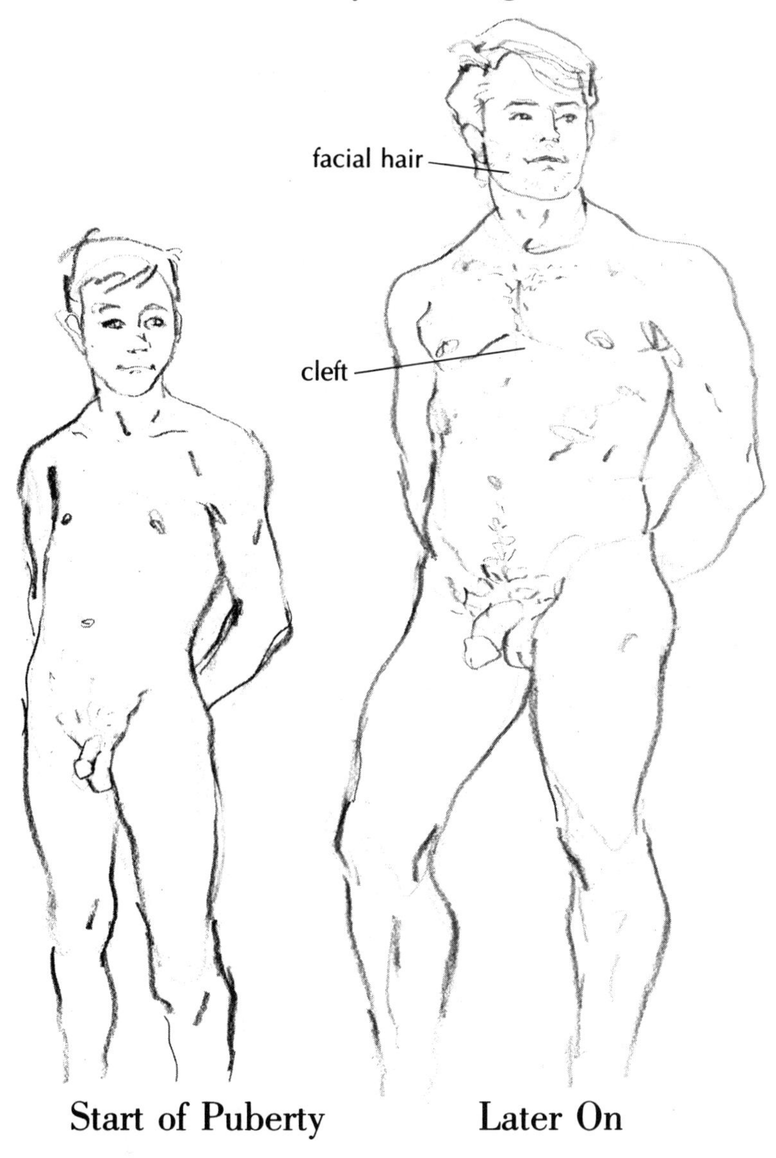

Boys change during puberty in many ways. At first they may grow in size and get pubic hair. As time goes on, their voices change, they grow facial hair, and they start to produce sperm.

These physical changes in boys affect their lives as much as the changes in girls affect girls' lives. During puberty both boys and girls are adjusting to changes that may make them feel insecure one day and proud the next.

Boys and girls have a hard time accepting themselves for who they are. Envy, jealousy, and insecurity are normal feelings that both boys and girls have many times during puberty, adolescence, and even adulthood.

One day you may walk up to the counter in the drugstore with a box of tampons in your hand and see a boy you know well behind the counter. "May I help you?" he asks. You feel your face flooded with embarrassment. What do you do? Just go ahead and make your purchase. It's not really such a big deal. Having your period is a natural part of life. If you act embarrassed, so will the boy. If you can handle it, the chances are that he can too.

Teachers and Other Grown-ups

Most teachers are aware of the changes boys and girls undergo during puberty. Usually they are understanding about specific problems, such as the embarrassment you may feel if your clothes get stained or the embarrassment a boy may feel if his new low voice squeaks in class.

At the same time teachers may be frustrated

with you if you give them a hard time. The changes and physical growth of puberty cause some boys and girls to start feeling so grown-up that they overly resist authority. Such kids may act like hotshots and be uncooperative in class, thereby irritating teachers. It is important for both kids and teachers to adjust and treat each other with respect.

Teachers should not tease you about your growth and bodily changes. Some male teachers and other grown men may think that it's okay to tease girls or touch them in a flirting sort of way, but it's not. This kind of behavior is wrong. Don't be led into thinking that it's funny or cute. If a male teacher or other adult teases you or touches you in a sexual way, tell him to stop. If he doesn't, tell someone in authority. You have the right to say no to such advances and to inform authorities of such behavior.

Yourself

During puberty you and your feelings toward yourself will change. The new womanly part of you will grow alongside the child in you. You took about a decade (ten years) to get this far. It will take about that much time again before you are an emotionally mature adult.

So go easy on yourself. Accept yourself as part

child and part woman, respecting and enjoying both parts. Be patient with your mood swings and confusions too, because they are to be expected as you try out different behaviors and have different experiences. It takes time to grow.

Getting your period is a special event in your life. It marks an important stage of personal growth, so let yourself feel proud, unique, and on your way. Congratulations!

Index

Page numbers in *italics* refer to illustrations.

About the Author

Jean Marzollo is the author of *Superkids* and other nonfiction books, and is a longtime contributor to *Parents* magazine with articles about childcare and childhood development. She has also written a wide range of titles for Dial, among them novels and picture books, and has won many honors for her writing. Ms. Marzollo is a graduate of the University of Connecticut and received an M.A. degree from the Harvard University Graduate School of Education. An editor as well as an author, Ms. Marzollo lives with her family in Cold Spring, New York.

About the Illustrator

Kent Williams is a noted illustrator living in New York City. In 1987 his work won the Silver Medal from the Society of Illustrators. This is his first book for Dial.